pleasure
exchange

Also by Cathryn Fox

PLEASURE PROLONGED
PLEASURE CONTROL

pleasure
exchange

CATHRYN FOX

red

AVON

An Imprint of HarperCollins*Publishers*

PLEASURE EXCHANGE. Copyright © 2008 by Cathryn Fox. All rights reserved. Printed in the United States of America. No part of this book may be used or reproduced in any manner whatsoever without written permission except in the case of brief quotations embodied in critical articles and reviews. For information address HarperCollins Publishers, 10 East 53rd Street, New York, NY 10022.

HarperCollins books may be purchased for educational, business, or sales promotional use. For information please write: Special Markets Department, HarperCollins Publishers, 10 East 53rd Street, New York, NY 10022.

FIRST AVON RED EDITION PUBLISHED 2008, REISSUED 2013.

Designed by Diahann Sturge

The Library of Congress has cataloged the original paperback edition as follows:

Fox, Cathryn
   Pleasure exchange / Cathryn Fox. — 1st ed.
      p. cm.
ISBN: 978-0-06-089857-1
I. Title.

PR9199.4.F69P555 2007
823'.92—dc22

                              2007020041

ISBN 978-0-06-226559-3

13 14 15 16 17   OV/RRD   10 9 8 7 6 5 4 3 2 1

To the Allure Authors, Vivi, Slyvia, Sasha, Myla, Lisa, and Delilah. Thank you for your friendship and support. You talented ladies continually inspire me!

Chapter 1

And here she thought things couldn't get any worse.

Surrounded by rowdy animal rights activists, journalist Cathleen Nichols rolled her eyes heavenward and wondered who the hell she'd pissed off in a past lifetime to deserve this. As if standing on a picket line outside the Iowa Research Center in a deluge of cold autumn rain with her makeup smeared and her hair plastered to her forehead wasn't enough to top off a perfectly shitty day, she'd spotted *him*.

The man who despised her.

The man who'd be thrilled to see her in such a predicament.

The same man who'd been starring in her fantasies for the past six months.

Oh hell.

Who knew the article she'd written about the Iowa Research Center's sexual experiments would draw so much attention? Negative attention, that is.

For him.

From behind the lobby doors, his piercing blue eyes sifted through the crowd and settled on her. *Oh boy!* Desire thrummed through her veins as their gazes collided. On her date rating scale this man scored a triple "A." Anywhere, anytime, anything. . . .

She'd been living across the courtyard from "not-so-nerdy" scientist Sam York for a little over six months. Except for the day he'd helped her carry in packing boxes, they'd barely spoken. She'd come to learn he dedicated his spare time to his work and didn't have much room in his life for other luxuries.

Luxuries like having her writhing beneath him on his king-sized bed. Her pulse leapt into action as she played out that provocative image. *Cripes! This wasn't the time to indulge in her rich sexual fantasies.*

She'd also come to learn that he spent many evenings at home, alone with his pet chimpanzee Rio, poring over research. And after a long tiring night of work, he'd sometimes forget to close his blinds when he undressed for bed.

Not that she watched and waited.

Not at all.

Not much anyway.

Her body fairly vibrated as she mentally indulged in the erotic slideshow. Sexual longing swamped her, liquid heat moistening the juncture between her legs. She swallowed, her throat suddenly the only dry part on her body.

Even though they were neighbors, they seldom crossed paths. On those rare occasions when they bumped into each other outside the building, they'd exchanged pleasantries. The soft warmth of his voice always pulled at her as his rich scent singed her blood and sent heat curling through her veins.

Sam usually left the house minutes before her but never failed to leave behind his spicy masculine aroma. It permeated the courtyard and seduced her senses. Cat inhaled, clinging to the enticing memory.

The restless crowd grew louder as they chanted and walked in circles around her. Camera crews milled about, filming the action for the evening news. Shaken from her fantasies, Cat glanced up to see Sam push past the lobby doors and step outside. Even though his mouth was set in a grim line, his captivating eyes still glimmered with dark sensuality.

With determined strides, Sam stalked forward. High over his head, his black umbrella bobbed like a buoy in the sea of people. More rankled than a caged animal, he weaved his way through the congestion and advanced toward her.

Shit!

Cat glanced at the clouds knitting together in the ominous, late afternoon sky. Where the hell was a bolt of lightning when she needed it?

A protestor's threatening voice boomed from behind. "Hey buddy, you're not going to get away with this. I'll personally see to it that you never experiment on that chimp of yours again."

Lord, she'd barely mentioned the chimp in the article yet activists had jumped all over that minor point, turning the parking lot into a circus sideshow.

Cat scanned the crowd and noted with mute interest how the majority of women seemed more enamored with Sam than angered. Eyes full of lust, they swarmed him, touching him with intimate recognition as he passed. They looked like a bevy of sharks ready to launch into a feeding frenzy. Cat snorted, suddenly annoyed. She knew exactly what those predators were interested in feasting on. It's not like she could blame them, really. When Sam's smoldering baby blues turned on her, it made her want to drop her panties, too.

The loud male protestor moved in beside her and continued his rant. His voice vibrated right through Cat, eliciting a shudder from deep within. Cat pressed her palms to her ears to block out the ungodly sound. She had one nerve left and the man was riding it.

She twisted sideways to glimpse the protestor who was as relentless as a pit bull and louder than a gaggle of preteens beheading a piñata. Well hell! Recognition hit like a high voltage jolt. It was none other than Eugene Letterman, a man who showed up at every protest, regardless of the cause.

As the camera turned on him, she cursed under her breath and tried not to feel as flustered as she felt. She looked heavenward. "Great. Kill me now." Cat linked her fingers together before she did something she'd regret. Like inflict the infamous protester with bodily harm.

Eugene Letterman. Otherwise known as Mr. Glory Hound around her office. An unemployed movie-star-wannabe working on turning his fifteen minutes of fame into a career.

Cat cringed as he spouted rude comments and made obscene gestures with his freakishly long middle finger. Cripes, his remarks were making this situation so much worse for Sam. Surely one little jab in the ribs wouldn't get her into too much trouble. The sudden, delightful image of Eugene dangling from a tree and Cat with a foot-long stick rushed through her mind. The visual made her grin.

She turned back to face Sam as he approached. A scowl etched his handsome face as he pinned her with a glare. Her smile dropped out of sight faster than Eugene Letterman after the cameras turned off. Starching her spine, she rooted her feet, jerked her chin up, and steeled herself. The look in Sam's eyes told her this was not going to be one of their pleasant courtyard exchanges.

It hadn't been her intention to piss Sam off or rattle animal rights activists. All she had wanted was to pen an article that would make her editor, Blain Grant, stand up and take notice of her writing skills. If she couldn't branch out and prove to Blain that she had the talent to write serious pieces, no New York newpapers would ever consider hiring her, and she'd never become a successful journalist like her father.

Her heart softened as she thought of her parents. It had been their dream to see their only daughter follow in her father's footsteps. The motor vehicle accident that had left her and her six older brothers parentless two years previously had acted like a catalyst for Cat, driving her to strive harder to move beyond tongue-in-cheek fluff articles to serious, hard-hitting news.

Just last week the ideal job had opened at the *Daily Press* in New York. In her quest to write journalistic pieces, she'd forwarded her resume along with a copy of her Iowa research article, the same article that had Sam riled. But without any other substantial experience or noteworthy editorials under her belt, she seriously doubted they'd give her a second glance, especially in such a fiercely competitive market.

Her editor gave all the hard-hitting news to Eric Hawkins, otherwise know as Hawk. Cat preferred to think he'd derived the nickname from his long pointed nose and beady eyes rather than his "Eye of the Hawk" column.

Cat's attention returned to Sam as he cut a path through

the crowd. She quickly palmed her hair and smoothed it from her face. Cat didn't know why she was so concerned about her appearance. Why bother trying to make herself look presentable for Sam York? He probably hated her, and honestly, she really didn't care how she looked to him.

Not at all.

Not much anyway.

Hell, who was she kidding? She wanted Sam. Upside down, inside out, but mostly on top. Perhaps it was her lack of dating or her inability to attract a decent guy that had her libido in an uproar and her mind conjuring up fantasies about her neighbor.

In truth, the downtown dating scene had left her colder than a snowman's balls. It hadn't taken her long to figure out she was a jackass magnet.

Cat wasn't looking for true love or any type of long-term relationship. After all, she had a career to concentrate on and was counting down the days until she could move to New York. The last thing she wanted was a man to keep her tied down in Iowa, preventing her from reaching her goal. She'd seen too many of her friends have babies and give up careers for a man only to end up broken and unhappy. That wasn't going to happen to her.

Nope, no way, not her. She hadn't spent years in journalism school to toss all that education out the window because some man gave her a panty-soaking smile, or to write fluff articles for a small time press, no matter how much she enjoyed it. With fierce determination, Cat had set her sights on *bigger and better*, as her father had always posed it. She planned on moving to New York where she could write articles that mattered. Articles that had value.

In the interim, however, a date or two with a nice guy would certainly be a welcome distraction. Unfortunately, she couldn't meet a nice guy if her life depended on it. Well, that wasn't entirely true. She'd met Sam York. And he certainly seemed nice enough. On many occasions, she'd watched him carry in groceries and hold the door for the elderly tenants in their complex. Call her old-fashioned but she liked it when a man showed a little chivalry. Small thoughtful gestures went a long way in her books.

Underneath his nerdy lab coat existed one hell of a sexy guy. Too bad he had more interest in his work and his chimp than her. And how did she remedy that small inconvenient problem? By writing an article on him and the lab's sexual experiments. Now he was lavishing her with lots of attention. Just not the kind she'd envisioned.

Brilliant!

Totally freaking brilliant!

The one man she wanted to get naked with didn't want to get naked with her.

She let out a long sigh.

Wasn't life a bitch like that?

The crowd tightened and moved forward as Sam stalked toward her. His eyes flared as they met hers. Shutting out the din of the protestors, she narrowed her focus and concentrated all her attention on Mr. Sexy Scientist.

He swept his arm through the masses and pulled her to him. "We need to talk." Good Lord, even laced with anger, the deep tenor of his sensuous voice seeped into her skin and filled her with longing. With effort, she fought down the urge to squirm.

Shielding her from the rain with his umbrella, he leaned forward, caging her between him and the protestors. He stood so close she could absorb the heat radiating from his flesh. His scent assailed her senses. She blinked a fat raindrop from her lashes and tipped her head to meet his eyes. A rush of sexual energy hit her as she allowed herself a moment to admire his roguish good looks. It baffled her that a guy this hot spent his nights alone. Especially seeing the way women reacted to him.

Maybe he was gay.

She pursed her lips. "Is there going to be yelling involved?"

A muscle in his jaw clenched as his frown deepened. "It's a high probability," he assured her.

She shrugged, her damp hair falling over her shoulders. "Okay, just checking."

Sam reached out and shackled her wrist. The warmth of

his skin chased the chill from her body. She kept pace as he negotiated them through the crowd and into the front lobby of his building. God, if he had this much passion when he was angry, she could only imagine how much he'd have when he was aroused. Damned if she didn't want to find out.

Once inside, he twisted around and leveled her with a glare. He muffled curses under his breath. "Do you have any idea. . ."

He stopped mid-sentence and hesitated. His simmering blue eyes flitted across her face before panning downward, registering every detail of her rain-soaked clothes. Had his gaze just lingered around the vicinity of her breasts?

So maybe he wasn't gay.

She acknowledged the flare of desire deep between her thighs as her body hummed in anticipation. She wondered if he could see the telltale hardening of her nipples beneath her wet, breast-hugging sweater.

She shivered, water dripping from her clothes and pooling at her feet. His features softened as his attention drifted back to her face. "We need to get you out of those clothes." Like a blanket of warmth, his seductive cadence heated her from the inside out. He brushed a damp lock from her cheek and tucked it behind her ear, an intimate gesture that sent shockwaves rocketing through her. A muscle in his jaw clenched. "Right now," he insisted, his voice sounding tight as he panned her body-molding clothes a second time.

A slow, lazy grin tugged at her mouth as her lust-drunk mind envisioned those strong hands disrobing her. Her gaze journeyed over his fine athletic body, taking in his low-slung scrubs and matching, short-sleeved, loose-fitting pale green top. She devoured every delicious detail as a curious tingle rushed through her bloodstream.

His brows knit together with concern. She recognized that look. It was the same motherly look of concern she'd seen her sister-in-law Sarah give her three-year-old nephew, Matt, when he'd come down with the flu a few months back.

"Before you catch pneumonia," he added.

The grin slipped from her face as her bliss disappeared. She resisted the urge to roll her eyes heavenward. *Gay.* Throwing her hands up, she nodded in understanding. "Of course, pneumonia. We wouldn't want that now, would we?"

He slipped his arm under hers and guided her to the security counter. "I keep an extra pair of scrubs in my lab. You can wear those, and then we need to talk."

Talk!

Didn't he know talking was overrated?

Especially when there were so many other things they could be doing.

As they moved through the foyer, across the wide expanse of marble floor, Sam angled his head and took in the wet erotic vision before him.

Cat Nichols.

He was convinced the drenched she-devil had been put on earth to try his patience. Had she never heard of a damn umbrella?

His blood ignited to near boiling as he allowed himself a brief luxurious moment to conjure up the image of him peeling off her soaked thigh-hugging jeans and breast-molding sweater.

Fuck. His damn future was at stake and all he could think about was sex. Terrific. That's what he got for burying himself in his work and going without the finer things in life for the last six months. And by finer, he meant Cat Nichols.

He commanded himself to redirect his thoughts as they approached the security counter. After he hastily signed her in and fitted her with a "visitor" pass, he watched the sway of her lush ass as she stepped onto the waiting elevator. He closed his eyes against the flood of heat gravitating south. Lord, what he'd do to cradle that hot little backside in his palms. Temptation like he'd never before experienced swamped him, prompting his dick into action.

He clenched his jaw and bit back a moan. The last thing he needed was a fucking hard-on in his unforgiving scrubs. A public display of his current aroused state ranked right up there with the time he'd gotten an erection during his seventh-grade gym class when Jessica Johnson had worn her short shorts. It was not one of his finer moments. It had been a long time since a woman had made him feel like a lusty, hormone-driven teen on date night. And here he'd thought he'd gotten control over those unexpected risings. Talk about the second coming!

A low growl rumbled from the depths of his throat and reverberated off the metal walls, despite his best efforts to stifle it.

Cat swatted her hair from her forehead and turned around to face him. "What was that?"

Ignoring her question, he jabbed the elevator button and leaned against the wall. He met her glance but wished he hadn't. Seductive green eyes dusted with tiny flecks of honey stared up at him. *Cat eyes.* Hence, the nickname, no doubt. Her blonde hair hung over slender shoulders, nestling against the gentle slope of her breasts. He'd just bet that sun-kissed color hadn't come from a bottle. His fingers clenched and unclenched as his gaze dropped to her waistband. Lust clawed to the surface as he perused her. She seemed completely unaware of her allure or how much she stirred his libido and fired his blood.

"Sam?"

The sweet melodic sound of her voice resonated through his body and pulled him back. He tried to hold onto his anger but it melted around the edges as his eyes met hers.

"Yeah?"

"What was that you said?"

13

"Nothing."

Shivering, she hugged herself and leaned toward him. Cat lifted one perfect brow. "I could have sworn you just said something."

He rolled one shoulder and hedged. "The elevator is old. It makes noises," he said, shifting his stance to hide his inflated body part.

Her arousing scent reached him. A delicious combination of sweet summer rain and succulent vine-ripened oranges. Of all things good and holy, that had to be the most seductive aroma he'd ever inhaled.

Shit, his goddamned cock just grew another inch.

Cat rubbed her palms up and down her arms. The gentleman in him urged him to offer his warmth. The man in him urged him to offer something a little farther south.

"Come here, you're freezing." Stepping into her personal space, he cradled her under his arms, warming her body with his. The snug contact created an instant air of intimacy. He felt a curious shift in his gut as she nuzzled against him and absorbed his heat.

The last few months had been hell. Total and utter hell. He'd barely been able to concentrate on his work knowing the sexy vixen lived mere minutes away in the condo across the courtyard. He wasn't sure whether it was a blessing or a curse that the positioning of their buildings provided him with a direct view of her bedroom when he stood inside his own.

He'd wanted to ask her out. In fact, he'd planned on it right after he completed his project and perfected his serum. Which would have been soon had she not written the damn article and drawn so much negative attention to him.

For the past six months his crazy schedule and deadline had left little room for extracurricular pleasures. He wasn't about to call on her until he could give her the attention she deserved, because judging by the number of men coming and going from her condo, Sam knew Cat Nichols demanded a lot of attention. And dammit, he wanted to be the guy to give it to her, not one of the six men who paraded in and out of her place at all hours while he was swamped with work.

Not that he watched and counted.

Not at all.

Not much anyway.

The truth was, Cat was exactly the kind of woman he dated. One who appeared to enjoy playing the field and didn't seem anxious to settle down or ask more from him than he could give.

The last thing he needed in his life was to get involved with a girl looking for a serious relationship, which made him wonder why he found the idea of Cat consorting with so many other men unsettling.

He berated himself for feeling so possessive toward her. His six-month boner and oxygen-starved brain had to be the reason he was feeling all peculiar inside. Christ, he really needed to get this girl out of his system. Surely once he appeased his body's primal urges, his thought processes would return to normal.

But he couldn't do that until he completed his project. Now, thanks to Cat's article, and the media's erroneous take on it, things at the lab were totally fucked up. Animal rights activists were pounding down his door, assuming the experimental serum would be tested on his pet chimpanzee, Rio. Due to the unexpected turn of events the Research Center's board of directors had halted his experiment, which prohibited him from completing his assignment. Even the press conference his Director, Reginald Smith, held hadn't assuaged protestors. Another round of curses lodged in his throat as he considered his dilemma.

He had to figure out a new game plan. Fast. But what? If only he could test the female libido enhancer on himself. Preliminary results had been a success with no side effects. He just had to run one more analysis before he could verify his findings to the Grant Governing Board. If he failed to make his deadline, his grant money would be allotted elsewhere. He couldn't let that happen. Too many people were counting on him.

He pulled Cat tighter in his arms as the perfect solution flashed through his mind like a lightning storm. Undoubtedly, the sexy wildcat who had messed things up would never agree to such a sinfully wicked plan.

Or would she?

His body buzzed as he entertained the idea. It was the perfect solution to his problem, really. He could complete his assignment and get the little spitfire out of his system.

The old elevator squealed and then jerked to a halt. As soon as the metal doors cleared he linked his fingers through hers, stepped out, and ushered her down the hall. He swiped his identification card through the electronic lock and pushed the lab door open.

"After you."

Cat offered a smile and walked past him, her sweet scent lingering behind, teasing and tormenting his libido. He banked his desires but his traitorous cock refused to obey.

Sam watched Cat catalogue her surroundings before making her way over to Rio. Without taking his eyes off her, Sam moved to his desk and pulled a pair of scrubs from his drawer. His lab wasn't huge, but it was big enough for his work station, his desk, and Rio's cage.

Hunkering down, Cat reached into the cage. Her hair spilled forward, brushing over her breasts. "Hey Rio, how are you, girl?" she asked. Gripping the bars, Rio rocked back and forth and made a hand gesture. Cat turned to face him. "What's she saying Sam?"

"She's saying she loves you." Which Sam thought was rather odd. Rio proved to be the jealous type. She hated when Sam brought women into the lab or into his condo. Perhaps

Rio felt a certain closeness with Cat from seeing her around the condo complex. Kind of the same way he did.

Oh boy!

It occurred to him that he was far more intrigued by Cat than he would have liked. She unearthed things in him he preferred to keep buried. Sam had had his fair share of physical relations with women but had avoided making deep connections. After his mother bailed, leaving a family behind, his father had a plethora of female companions. They'd hang around for a while, long enough for Sam to form a bond, then just like his mother, when something *bigger and better* came along, they would up and leave without warning.

Sam did a mental reminder of his rules. Never get too interested and never let them get too close because in the end, all women he got emotionally attached to ended up walking out.

One perfect brow arched. "You taught her sign language?" Cat climbed to her feet.

Sam shrugged. "Yeah." He pointed to the small bathroom. "You can get changed in there. I'll make coffee."

He took pleasure in the sight of her sweet backside as she moved across the room. At the sound of the door clicking shut behind her, Sam went to work on making a fresh pot of coffee. He turned his attention to Rio while waiting for it brew.

Crouched on his knees, he petted her. "What are we

going to do, girl? If I can't finish the assignment, I can kiss my career and any future grants good-bye." Rio signed that she loved him. Sam laughed. "I love you, too." Lips flapping, Rio grabbed the metal bars on her cage and pulled, giving Sam a message. "Yes, I know, I promised you a bigger cage, too." A fresh wave of anger ripped through him. He fisted his hands and clenched his jaw. "That damn article has complicated everything." He stroked Rio's back, nuzzled his face next to hers, and then stalked back over to the coffee pot.

"These things are pretty comfortable."

The sound of Cat's voice brought his attention back around to her. He twisted sideways and made the mistake of panning the length of her body. There was something very sensual about a woman in a pair of scrubs, he decided.

As his gaze caressed her curves, anger once again segued to desire, leaving him warm and wanting. Cuffs rolled up at the ankle, her pants rode low on flared hips. Underneath her thin top she wore no bra, gifting him with a view of perfect round peaks. Eyes fixated on her sweet angles, he tried not to stare, but her gentle slopes proved too much of a distraction. His fingers itched, forcing him to fight his natural inclination to touch her. Christ, if she'd removed her damp bra, he could only bet she'd disposed of her panties too. Fire licked over his thighs. Oh hell! He gulped air as his thoughts scattered like his lab rats when the lights flicked on.

"Coffee smells good."

Right. Coffee. Censoring his thoughts, he turned from her probing gaze and filled her mug. His knuckles brushed her skin as he handed it to her. Soft. So very soft. Like a kitten's fur. He wondered if she purred too.

"Have a seat; let's talk." He tried to keep his voice level, but it came out harsher than he intended.

She raised one hand in a halting motion. "Before you start yelling, I want to apologize."

He opened his mouth to speak, but she cut him off.

"First, hear me out." Cat grabbed a chair, tipped her mug, and took a tiny sip of her coffee. "I heard what you said to Rio and I really am sorry, Sam. The article wasn't meant to draw negative attention to your experiments. I just wanted to break away from fluff articles and show my editor what I'm capable of."

Sam's head came up with a start. It surprised him that she considered her work fluff. He loved her humorous "Cat on the Prowl" column. A satirical take on "men, mating and masturbating" as she put it. On many mornings her column was the topic of conversation around the watercooler.

"Fluff articles?"

She blew out a breath and continued. "If I ever want to move up the food chain at the paper, I need to start writing serious news. Without substantial experience or noteworthy editorials, no one is going to look twice at me." Cat took another sip of coffee and blinked up at him. "So you see Sam, I respect your work. It was never my intention to upset you or lead protestors to believe you were going to hurt Rio. I, for one, understand the need for testing but never thought for a minute you'd do anything to harm her. I've seen the way you care for her."

The last shreds of anger dissipated as he met her apologetic eyes. He understood the inner drive to succeed. He had that drive himself.

"So I've been giving it a lot of thought." She leaned forward, her plunging neckline affording him a view of her creamy cleavage, fueling his imagination. In that instant, he knew there was nothing he could do to deter his cock from rising to the occasion and tenting his pants. The gentleman in him urged him to look the other way. The man in him decided at this particular moment, manners were overrated.

His mind careened off track. Desire stabbed through him. He indulged his wayward thoughts as he envisioned his mouth wrapped around one perfect, pink areola, sucking, nibbling, and licking until she cried out in painful bliss. *Sweet mother of God and all good things holy!* His sinful thoughts were paving him a path straight to Hell.

"I've figured out a way I can help you finish the experiment."

He transferred his thoughts back to the situation. "Help?" He poured a generous amount of cream into his coffee and met her at the table.

She cleared her throat before speaking. Her voice thinned to a whisper as she proceeded. "Yeah, me in exchange for the chimp." With a quick nod, she motioned to Rio.

Had she read his mind?

Blood racing, he came up short. His knees nearly went right out from under him, causing him to spill his coffee. Suddenly it took effort to stand. He pulled out a chair and lowered himself into it. He met her gaze from across the table.

She had to be kidding.

He paused and cocked his head, assessing her. They stared at each other for a long quiet moment. He furrowed his brow, unable to believe her offer.

"Are you serious?"

Her sensuous mouth twisted into a frown, clearly indicating her silent apology. She wrapped her slender hands around her mug and blew out a slow breath. "I got you into this mess, it's the least I could do to get you out."

He got quiet for a moment as he mulled over her offer. Did she have any idea what she was getting herself into? Any idea of how they'd have to test the serum. Provocative images of how he'd like to test her responses to the libido enhancer made his pulse rate kick up a notch. He bit back a low growl of longing as his desire mounted.

He threaded his fingers through his hair and kept his voice controlled. "Do you have any idea what this entails?"

She nodded, dark lashes opening wide over come-hither

eyes. "Testing a female libido enhancer," she rushed out, leaning toward him. He caught another whiff of her delectable orange scent.

Sam had to admit, right now there were two things he wanted. One, to complete his assignment on time, and two, Cat Nichols. Not necessarily in that order. Damned if she wasn't offering him a way to have both. He'd never mixed work and pleasure before. The two had never gone hand in hand. Until now.

"Cat, do you understand what you'd have to do to help me?"

"Not exactly," she confessed.

Sam leaned back in his chair and stretched his legs. Warmth coiled through him as his calf brushed hers. She didn't flinch, nor did she pull away. What she did do was shift in her chair, allowing more of her leg to brush his.

It took all his effort to force his arousal-fogged brain back to their conversation. "First, we have to test and record your sexual responses to stimuli without the enhancer. Then we wait twenty-four hours, give you the serum, and test your responses again."

Her eyes darkened. "Sam?" she asked, her voice a little uneven, a little raspy. "What stimuli?"

He angled closer, gauging her reactions. He spent a long moment just looking at her before he answered in a soft tone, "Me."

"I see." The seductive lilt to her voice made his body tighten. Twirling a damp lock through her fingers, she stared into the depths of her coffee mug, her expression a mixture of apprehension and intrigue.

"Second thoughts?"

He watched her throat work as she swallowed. "I'll do whatever it takes to get the media off your back and help you complete your experiment, even if that means taking Rio's place." She gestured toward Rio and signed the words I love you.

Sam smiled as he watched the exchange. The way she'd taken to his chimp, and vice versa, surprised and pleased him. Probably a hell of a lot more than it should have.

"The thing is, Cat. I wasn't testing the enhancer on Rio."

Her head came up with a start. "No?"

"No. It's not Rio you're replacing, it's her." Jerking his thumb in the air, he pointed to Bonnie, his lab rat. "I was going to test the serum on Bonnie, but the Board of Directors halted all animal experiments until the protest died down."

Cat's eyes opened wide. "Oh?"

He leaned into her and grinned. "You'll be taking the place of my lab rat. Does that change things for you?" he said, giving her a way out, hoping like hell she didn't take it.

She drew a shaky breath, slid her tongue over her bottom lip, and swiped away a raindrop that slipped from her bangs. She closed her hand over his, a combination of heat and desire flickering in her eyes.

"Of course not, Sam. Why would you think that?" she asked, her voice darkly seductive. Suddenly, the air around them changed as sexual energy arced between them.

Heat pooled in his thighs as her warm breath wafted across his face. A slow grin curled his lips. The look in her eyes spoke volumes. Her needs and desires matched his. *Hot damn!* His mind began racing, plotting, and tweaking the finite details of his experiment.

"One question, Sam."

"Yeah?"

She grinned. "Were *you* the stimuli for the rat too?"

A low chuckle rumbled in his throat. "No."

Her eyes darkened. Her voice turned low, breathy. "Must be my lucky day."

He smiled. Damned if he didn't like a woman who made no bones about what she wanted. He was quickly learning that Cat Nichols wasn't the kind of woman to play coy or hard to get, like most other women he knew. With her, there were no cat-and-mouse games. And he found that damn refreshing.

He squeezed her hand, bringing passion to her green eyes. All teasing disappeared from his voice. "Not yet it isn't."

He watched the way her body trembled, despite the warm, dry clothes.

"So what do you say?" Her voice sounded edgy. "Do you accept my apology and my proposition?"

He opened his mouth to reply when reality hit him full force. It went completely against protocol to test the serum on humans before written approval. If his Director got wind of it, he'd kick Sam's ass to the curb. But if he wanted to prove his findings to the Grant Governing Board and secure future grants, he'd have to break protocol. Who knew how much time it'd take for protestors to settle down and testing to begin again, and since time was something he didn't have. . . .

He scrubbed his hand over his chin and considered his options. There really was only one solution. To make sure what happened in the research room, stayed in the research room.

Could he trust Cat to abide by those rules? If he wanted to complete this assignment and get the little wildcat out of his system, he had no choice.

He narrowed his gaze. "This won't make it into your paper?" he asked.

"Never." There was nothing in her voice to suggest otherwise.

He glanced into her seductive bedroom eyes. Heat curled a lazy path to his loins. Blonde curls had begun to dry and spring upward to frame her honey-tanned skin. Beautiful.

"Well . . . ?" she inquired.

Oh yeah, he planned on taking her up on her offer alright. He had many reasons to accept, but right now most of them had nothing to do with the experiment.

Chapter 2

Darkness had settled over the city as Sam parked his jeep outside his condo and climbed from the driver's seat. He stole a quick glance at his watch and hurried up the walkway. Damn, he hated to be late for anything, especially a sexy experiment with a woman who'd been getting under his skin for the last six months.

As he pushed open his front door, his stomach grumbled, reminding him that in his quest to make the research room perfect for Cat, he'd stayed late and skipped dinner.

Kicking off his shoes, Sam made his way to his fridge and grabbed a cold piece of leftover chicken. As he bit into it, he scooped up a napkin and looked at the wall clock. With only twenty minutes to spare, he still needed to shower and shave before calling on Cat.

Cat.

Just the mere thought of her had his body reacting with urgent demands. In less than an hour he'd have her all alone in the research room and he'd finally have a chance to sample her lush body and get her out of his system. His cock throbbed just thinking about tasting and kissing her gorgeous, plump lips.

Both sets.

He practically salivated as his mind shifted through all the mouthwatering ways he planned on devouring her.

A strange primal yearning rolled through him as he thought about moving beyond pleasant courtyard exchanges to a deeper level of intimacy while testing Cat's responses to sexual stimulation.

His sexual stimulation.

Something about the emotions Cat pulled from him really threw him off balance. Sam had always remained cool, confident, distant, and detached with the women he'd had sex with.

Sex was just that. Sex. Nothing more, nothing less. Insert tab A into slot B. Repeat if necessary. Simple good clean fun between two emotionally unattached people. At least that was the way it had always been. Sam had always kept a modicum of distance with the female gender and never let himself get too involved.

Nor did he plan to.

Tugging his shirt from his waistband, he pulled it off and

tossed it into his bedroom as he rounded the corner to the bathroom.

The doorbell sounded. A muscle in Sam's jaw clenched, suddenly concerned that Cat had stopped by to tell him she'd changed her mind. Of course, this would be disastrous for his six-month hard-on, not to mention his inability to complete his assignment.

He swallowed his last bite of chicken, tracked back to the door, and pulled in a fortifying breath. He eased the door open and relaxed, realizing how tense he'd felt only moments before.

His heart softened and filled with love as he came face-to-face with the most beautiful girl in the world. A girl who had taken up residency in his heart one month previous.

Sam had been mistaken earlier. There was one girl he didn't keep a modicum of distance with, after all. The first time their eyes had met, she'd broken through his defenses.

Composing himself, Sam reached out to her. In a protective manner, he took her little body into his embrace and planted a gentle, heartfelt kiss on her rosy cheek.

He pitched his voice low. "I wasn't expecting you," he murmured, cradling Samantha, his one-month-old goddaughter, in his arms.

Kale clapped him on the shoulders. "Hey Sam, how's it going?" Kale asked, stepping into the condo after relinquishing his sleeping daughter.

Sam leaned out his door and briefly looked around. His eyes skirted the parking lot. "Where's Erin?" With the butt of his heel, he shut the door and faced Kale.

"Resting." Kale yawned and brushed a gentle finger over Samantha's cheek. He nodded his chin toward the bundle of joy in Sam's arms. "Our little girl here fussed all night so I thought I'd give mommy a break and bring her over to visit with her favorite godfather."

Sam took the baby's hand in his. Tiny fingers curled around his index. "Well, I'm glad you did." Samantha stirred and opened her big blue eyes. Sam's heart tightened. He hugged her against his bare chest as emotions rushed through him like a runaway freight train. As he cradled her, Samantha's chubby little body molded against his. The fresh scent of baby powder reached his nostrils.

Sam dipped his head. A few sprigs of Samantha's dark hair tickled his cheek. "Hey sweetheart," he murmured, brushing his lips over her forehead. Christ, who would have thought that such a little thing like her could arouse so many foreign feelings in him?

Sam took a breath and met Kale on the sofa. He lowered himself and propped his feet up, carefully positioning Samantha's head in the crook of his arm, securing her against him. Angling his head, Sam read Kale's body language, taking in the tension and concerned look on his face.

Like himself, Kale was usually laid back and relaxed. Sam detected none of those carefree qualities in his friend tonight. Something was up. "Now tell me why you're really here," Sam said.

Kale chuckled and shifted to face Sam. "You know me too well."

Sharing the same interests, Sam and Kale had become instant friends when Kale had taken a position at the lab and married Sam's friend and coworker, Erin Shay. Well, it was now Erin Alexander.

Sam's eyebrow shot up. "What's up?"

Kale mimicked Sam's position, propping his feet up. Without preamble, he got right to the point. "I was concerned about your deadline. With protestors breathing down your neck and the Board of Directors temporarily shutting down your project, how are you going to test the libido enhancer and prove your finding to the Grant Governing Board on time?"

"I've got it under control," Sam assured him.

Kale cocked a brow and scrubbed his hand over his chin. The poor guy looked like he hadn't shaved in a week.

"Yeah? Care to elaborate," Kale probed.

Sam rolled one shoulder, shifted Samantha in his arms, and offered no further explanation.

Kale narrowed his gaze, scrutinizing him, his voice taking on a serious edge. "From what I understand you have no options, Sam. Our Director wants the serum perfected as much as the rest of us, but you know bad press means big trouble and a skittish Board of Directors. You and I both know the Research Center counts on the grant money, but the Director also informed me the Board has made their decision and it's completely out of his hands. Until the bad press dies down, your project is on hold."

Sam clenched his jaw as his mind sorted through matters. The way Sam saw it, since he was dealing with two completely different boards, he could finish his assignment, present it to the Grant Governing Board, secure his grant, and the Board of Directors would be none the wiser.

"I don't have time for the protest to die down. You know what these activists are like." Sam shook his head and blew out a frustrated breath. "Greenpeace has nothing on them. They get something in their heads and won't listen to reason. Even if Cat wrote another article clarifying things, it wouldn't matter."

"Cat?" Kale asked, his voice a mixture of curiosity and concern.

"The reporter who started this," Sam offered.

"The one who moved into Erin's old condo?"

Working to keep his face expressionless, Sam nodded. The less Kale knew the better. If this plan backfired, he didn't want Kale going down with him.

"I see," Kale said, his eyes assessing Sam.

Fidgeting under his scrutinizing gaze, Sam slanted

his head and glanced at the clock. Kale watched the movement.

"Am I keeping you?"

"I have a date." Sam paused, wondering why the word "date" popped into his mind.

Kale rose and gathered Samantha into his arms. "A date? Seems to me you haven't had one of those in awhile. Erin will be happy to hear that. She's worried that you've been working too hard."

Sam stood and crossed his arms, immediately missing Samantha's warmth, suddenly feeling very . . . lonely.

He donned his professional face and met Kale's glance. Both Erin and Kale had entrusted him with this experiment when they took extended leave to stay home with Samantha. He wasn't going to make them regret the decision. "I will see this project to completion, Kale, no matter what it takes."

"Be careful, Sam. The Board halted your experiment. If you get caught doing what I think you're doing and our Director finds out, you can kiss your job goodbye."

Sam clapped his friend on the back. "Everything is under control, Kale," he assured. "Now I have to go, I'm running late."

"One more thing, Sam."

"What?"

A bemused expression crossed his face. "You might

want to distinguish the difference between a date and an experiment."

"You're doing what with whom?"

Cat hushed her best friend and neighbor, Jen, and rushed around her condo looking for her sexy, hot red pumps, or "fuck-me-shoes" as Jen preferred to call them.

God, it had been so long since she'd worn high heels it'd be a damn miracle if she made it through the night without tripping. With the way her luck was going she'd likely fall and break something vital to the experiment. For a brief moment she wondered if her ass was vital. Surely it had to be. If she broke her neck or her ass, then she'd never get to hold up her end of the deal, which would be horrible for Sam. Of course, Sam's project really was her main concern. Not her overactive libido or the way it was screaming at her to answer her bodily urges with a guy who'd been a reoccurring character in her erotic dreams. No, it had nothing at all to do with that. Girl Scouts honor.

Cat popped a wedge of orange into her mouth and pressed her fingers to her lips. "Shhh . . . he's going to be here any minute and I don't want him to hear you."

Jen dropped to her knees, peered under the sofa, and produced the missing shoes. "Cat, I can't believe you're going to be a damn lab rat." She coiled the straps around her fingers and swung them like a pendulum.

Neither could Cat. It was all she'd been able to think about since suggesting it earlier that day. That and how Sam planned on using himself as *stimulus.*

"Since you insist on going through with this, you might need one of these. Two if you're really lucky." Jen grabbed a couple of small foil packages from her purse and slipped them into Cat's handbag. "This is a *condom.*" She stretched out the last word. "It goes on the man's penis—"

Cat swallowed her orange and cut Jen off with a glare. "Just because I haven't used one in ages, doesn't mean I forgot what it's for. Besides, I won't need it. Sam is testing my responses; we're not testing his."

"And you don't think he's going to get just a little turned on while he's doing that?"

She could dream, couldn't she?

Jen's eyes opened wide, like she'd just won the state lottery, and she giggled like a schoolgirl. "Do you think he's going to give you multiple orgasms? The serum is to increase the female libido. Surely he's going to have to record your responses during a climax, or two, or maybe three if you're really lucky."

God, she hoped so. The truth was she had no idea what Sam had in store for her.

"I'm sure it won't come to that." Cat grabbed the heels and slipped into them. She stood in front of her hall mirror and glanced at her jeans and blouse. She'd agonized all evening on what to wear. A slinky dress or jeans? In the end she'd settled for jeans. After all, Sam was conducting an experiment, not taking her on a date.

Cat studied her profile a moment longer. "What do you think of the shoes? Overkill?"

"Not if you're screaming fuck me." A wry grin curled Jen's mouth, one brow rising inquisitively. "Are you screaming, fuck me, Cat?"

As a fourth-year psychology student, Jen had a habit of overanalyzing any situation. Cat turned, checking the angle from the back. "Cut the analysis crap, Jen. I told you this isn't about sex. I'm just helping Sam with the experiment. It's the least I can do." She smoothed her hand over a few temperamental curls, teasing them down.

Jen snorted. "Who are you trying to convince of that, me or you?"

A knock on the door drew their attention. Jen grinned and whispered in Cat's ear, "Maybe if you're really good, he'll let you play with his monkey."

Cat stifled a chuckle. "You are so bad."

Jen leaned against the wall. "Me? Bad? I'm not the one playing sex games with Romeo."

"Romeo?"

"Come on, Cat. Sam has reached out and touched more women than Hallmark."

Cat planted her hands on her hips. "I've been living here

for six months and I haven't seen him with anyone but that cute little chimp of his."

"That's because he's been buried in a project. Before that . . . well, let's just say before that women were lining up like he was an amusement ride."

Taking pause, Cat remembered the way the women on the picket line swarmed him, touching him with familiarity. Did they know him on an intimate level? Had they all gone for a wild ride on his joystick? Jen had to be wrong. Sam really didn't strike her as the playboy type at all.

Cat spoke in a hushed tone. "But he's such a gentleman and he seems so sweet," she countered.

Jen lowered her voice to match Cat's. "Oh he is sweet, Cat. Candy apple sweet. All six foot two of him. Or so I've been told." Jen gave her a wink. "And he's also a gentleman. Ladies first, if you know what I mean."

Cat crinkled her nose, trying to wrap her head around the idea that Sam was a playboy. "He's so nurturing, though. Have you ever seen him with Rio?"

"He's nurturing all right." Jen picked up Cat's orange, tossed a piece into her mouth, and handed the last wedge to Cat. "From what I hear he'll nurture multiple orgasms right out of you." Jen crinkled her brow. "Come to think of it, maybe you're not so crazy after all. Let me know where I can sign up to be a lab rat," she teased. "It's been awhile since I had multiple . . . *anything*."

Cat shot Jen a silencing look, tamped down the odd churning in her stomach, and walked to the door. It really shouldn't bother her to find out Sam had his own harem of women. It wasn't like they were in an intimate relationship, nor was she even entertaining the idea. Not for a split second. He could date as many women as he wanted. It didn't matter one measly iota to her.

Which had her wondering why the image of Sam as the main carnival attraction left her feeling very disconcerted.

Pushing back the surge of jealousy, Cat furrowed her brow and pressed her fingers to her lips in warning. "Be good and play nice." She tossed her orange slice into her mouth, wrapped her palm around the doorknob, and twisted.

Jen shook her curly black locks from her shoulders. "Only if you'll be bad and share the details."

Cat ignored her friend and pulled her door open. One word came to mind as she caught his sexy, bad-boy grin.

Stimuli.

No, that's a lie. Two words came to mind. *Stimuli. Me. Now.* Or was that three?

As she took in the handsome man before her, she gasped. She actually gasped. And he heard it. Good Lord. One look from him and she turned into a speechless sex nymph.

Sam's sun-bleached hair looked damp from a recent shower. His scent, an aphrodisiacal combination of soap, shampoo, and one hundred percent grade A male, curled around her, drawing her into a cocoon of need and desire. She wondered what he wore underneath that long leather trench coat. Professional, easy-to-remove, loose-fitting scrubs or those aged, faded jeans of his that had her drooling like an overheated Saint Bernard, and, on more than one occasion, had had her doing a few intimate, solo experiments of her own.

With effort she spoke. "Hi," she pushed that one word out past the lump lodged in her throat. "I'm all wet . . . set. I mean set. I'm all set," she repeated like a babbling idiot.

Good Lord.

If he caught her slip, he ignored it and for that Cat was grateful. Cat grabbed her coat, shrugged it on, and hitched her handbag high on her shoulder.

If this were a date, she would have played it cool and kept him waiting, but it wasn't a date. Why did she constantly have to remind herself of that? Because Sam York had never shown any interest in her as a woman before and right now he thought of her as nothing more than a lab rat.

"Sorry I'm late. I had a few last-minute things at the lab to take care of." He looked past her shoulder. "Hey, Jen. How's it going?"

Jen looked like she was about to swoon when he gifted her with one of his panty-soaking smiles. Cat couldn't blame her, really. It had taken all her strength and two locked knees to keep herself upright.

"Hey, Sam. Things are good. Where's Rio?" Jen pushed

off the wall and hooked her thumbs through her belt loops.

Sam turned sideways to let Cat through the doorway. "She's at the lab."

"If you ever need a sitter, I'd be more than happy to play with your . . . *monkey*," Jen offered.

Cat gulped. *Oh, my God.* Her orange rose from her stomach and lodged in her throat. Jesus, she was going to kill Jen when she got back.

One sexy brow cocked as Sam slanted his head and shot Jen a glance. "I'll keep that in mind."

Cat twisted around, glared at her grinning friend, and cast a look that suggested her days were numbered as she gripped the knob and pulled her door closed.

Glancing around, Cat noted that darkness had settled over the city. A warm, white light drifted out from the condo and spilled onto the porch. Sam dipped his head and looked at her, a sparkle simmering in his baby blues.

"She was talking about Rio, right?"

His velvety smooth voice bombarded her body with rich, evocative sensations. The tips of his sun-drenched hair blew in the gentle night breeze, framing his strong chiseled face. God, he was so beautiful. Her heart did a weird little dance, the Macarena if she had to guess.

She swallowed, her insides turning to putty. A wayward lock fell over his eyes. She linked her fingers together, resisting the pull to brush it from his forehead.

Cat suppressed a shiver of longing and let out a heavy breath. It formed a cloud in the cool air. She waved a dismissive hand and dodged the question. "I think she's been studying too hard. Just ignore her." Nodding to the parking lot, she brought their conversation back to the night ahead. "My car or yours?"

Sam fished his keys out of his coat. The enticing scent of leather reached her nostrils. What was it about a man in leather that made her hotter than suicide salsa? Well, not just any man. *This man.*

"I'll drive." Strong arms circled her shoulders and pulled her in tight, tight enough that every inch of his sculpted body touched hers. Warmth spread over her skin. Lord, it felt so good when he touched her and held her in such a protective manner. Growing up in a houseful of guys, Cat had fought for her independence. Most men made her feel smothered, yet around Sam she didn't experience any of those unpleasant feelings at all.

He slanted his head and offered her one of his incredible smiles. Cat felt her body grow moist and her knees turn to pudding. A sudden breeze rushed through the parking lot and ruffled his hair. The light wind drifted over her warm face and helped ease the heat inside her.

Shrouded in darkness, she hurried her footsteps to keep pace as they crossed the unlit parking lot. Her "fuck-me-shoes" tapped a steady rhythm and cut through the silence enveloping them. So far, so good. She hadn't fallen and broken her ass, or any other vital parts. Fortunately, the rain had subsided, leaving a fresh autumn scent in the breezy evening air and the ground nice and dry for walking in heels.

Sam opened the passenger side door for her. She stepped away from the circle of his arms and immediately missed his touch. She made herself comfortable in his sporty Jeep as he climbed behind the wheel and maneuvered them out of the parking lot.

"Sam?" She may have appeared calm on the outside but their close proximity rattled her more than dice in a Yahtzee cup. Chaos erupted inside her as a tremor of awareness made her quiver in the most interesting places.

"Hmmm?"

She wrinkled her nose. "Are you going to hook me up to electrodes?"

He grinned and shook his head. "No need to."

"Oh." Folding her hands on her lap, she nodded and focused on the dark road ahead. Out of her peripheral vision, she caught him staring at her.

"You sound disappointed."

She faced him. "No, it's not that. I'm just wondering how you're going to record my responses to your," she swallowed before completing the sentence, "*stimuli.*"

Sam's bad-boy grin turned wicked. "Trust me, Cat. Tomorrow night after we enhance your sensitivity, you'll be able to *feel* the different responses in your body." He leaned closer, until his mouth was only a tongue flick away from hers. "And so will I."

Oh yeah, he had every intention of *feeling* her responses because the minute he got her alone in the research room he planned on sliding his hands over every delicious speck of her sweet-scented bare skin. He'd waited far too long as it was.

Twenty minutes later, he pulled his Jeep into his assigned parking spot and glanced at her profile, soaking in her beauty. He was so aware of her, her every breath, her every movement. Watching her for the past six months had left him feeling as though he'd known her for a lifetime when, in fact, he didn't really know her very well at all. Tonight that was about to change. They were going to get to know each other. *Intimately.*

His eyes caressed her face. Long blonde curls framed her high cheekbones and billowed over slender shoulders. A dark curtain of thick black lashes flickered over her green eyes. Sam shifted in his seat, giving her his full attention. Hands folded she stared straight ahead, her expression unreadable. He couldn't tell whether nervousness or excitement stirred her soul. He hoped for the latter.

He raised an inquisitive brow. "You sure you want to do this?"

She turned to face him. Her head nodded, repeatedly. "Yes. Of course."

Sam let out a breath he hadn't realized he was holding. When Cat moistened her lips, it took every ounce of control he possessed not to brush his own tongue over her mouth, to feel if her lips were as lethally soft as they looked. He ached to taste her, to take pleasure in her plump mouth moving under his. God, he wanted her. Inside out, upside down, but mostly underneath.

Hell, it was all he'd been able to think about for the last few months. He clenched his jaw, scrubbed a hand over his chin, and drew a breath. Later, he promised himself. *Later.*

"What's the game plan?" she asked. Her voice sounded tight.

"Once we get inside, I'll test your responses to stimuli, without the serum." His cock throbbed in anticipation. *Down boy!* Fuck, he needed to get control of himself. What was it about her that had his dick in a constant state of flux?

His glance flickered over her knee-length coat. His imagination kicked into high gear as he visualized himself ridding her body of the unnecessary barrier of clothes that separated skin from skin.

Green eyes came alive with curiosity. Her chest heaved, drawing his attention downward. "How exactly do you plan on doing that?"

He guessed that question had been on her inquisitive mind

all day. He pitched his voice low and sidled closer. "First, I'll have to remove your clothes." He reached out and touched her coat. With slow, sinuous movements, he fingered the soft material.

Hanging on his every word, she arched forward to meet him. Mouth poised open, her breathing grew shallow. Seductive cat eyes turned one shade darker. Her feminine aroma mingled with the faint scent of oranges and saturated the cab of the Jeep, stoking the fire smoldering inside him.

"Then . . . we'll . . ." He stopped talking. Primitive need compelled him to brush the pad of his thumb over her moist painted lips. He took a moment to dwell on the softness. He nearly came unhinged as the smooth texture of her skin sent heat charging to his cock. She didn't seem to mind his intimate touch. In fact, a sexy pink hue suffused her skin as desire flitted across her face.

"Yes?" she probed, urging him on. "Then what?" A mixture of curiosity and excitement lingered in her tone.

A smile pulled at his mouth. Hot damn. He loved how much she was into him. *Into this game.* It suddenly occurred to him how thrilled he was that she wanted him. How much that mattered to him.

Christ, maybe this game would prove to be more dangerous than he anticipated. There was something very irresistible about Cat Nichols. He swallowed. Hard. Suddenly feeling off kilter.

The thing was, he genuinely liked Cat and wanted her, no, *needed* her with an intensity and urgency like he'd never before experienced. And that frightened him.

Catching him off guard, Cat reached out, closed her hand over his, and squeezed. The feel of her warm skin pushed away his reserve as his mind took him on a journey of the ways he planned on taking her.

Anticipation rushed through his bloodstream, generating warmth and need, scattering his thoughts. His gaze panned her face and met with eyes full of dark passion. Fuck, he couldn't wait to get her alone, to feel her sensuous body beneath his. A restless ache stirred his dick, suddenly making his seated position most unbearable.

Needing to feel her under him, he deliberately leaned across her and pulled open her door handle. With Cat pinned beneath him, he pressed against her and absorbed her tremble. He felt her warm breath on the back of his neck. The next time he trapped her body under his, she'd be naked, he silently vowed. Naked, wet, and writhing. His cock pulsed and throbbed in anticipation.

He let out a slow breath and straightened in his seat. "I have a better idea. Instead of telling you what I plan on doing, why don't you come with me and I'll show you instead."

"Okay." Her voice sounded breathless.

Sam climbed from the driver's seat and circled the Jeep to

meet her. He snaked his arm around her slender shoulders, holding her close, offering his warmth in the cool night air. She felt so good in his arms, so natural, like it was where she was meant to be.

Dark lashes fluttered in appreciation for that small gesture. Something about those honest, honey-flecked eyes and the warm, wanting way they gazed at him sucked him under like a tidal wave, pulling him into an emotional place he had no intentions of going. They'd have their fun, then part as friends. Sam never let anyone get too close. Heartbreak wasn't an option.

Sam tightened his embrace. Cat's smile widened. Her smile was more sweet than seductive and could undoubtedly disarm an entire S.W.A.T team. He felt an odd twist in his stomach and quickly pushed it aside.

A golden halo from the street light fell over her as he escorted her into the main lobby. She looked like an angel who'd fallen from the sky.

Sam pulled open the door and motioned for her to enter. She always seemed so pleased yet surprised by his gentlemanly gestures. Tenderness stole over him. He furrowed his brow trying to understand what it was about her that spawned such peculiar emotions inside him. He'd never moved past a sexual relationship before, always keeping things superficial. So what suddenly compelled him to think about lazy afternoons, long nights, and lasting relationships?

Unnerved by the direction of his thoughts, he banished them to the far corners of his mind.

A few minutes later, after signing in and taking the elevator to the top floor, he guided her down a narrow hallway to the research room.

Cat's eyes darted between the sign over the door and him. She tossed him a perplexed frown. By small degrees, her body tightened. "We're not going to your lab?"

They were playing in his territory now and he planned on taking full advantage of it. "Nope, we're taking this experiment into the research room. It's much better . . ." he paused, searching for the right word, "equipped for what I have planned."

He pushed open the door and ushered her inside. He studied her expression and watched her shoulders relax as she glanced around. In an attempt to vacate any clinical feel, Sam had stayed late, setting the mood for seduction. Music, the same music he'd often heard blaring from Cat's open condo window, drifted in from a corner speaker instantly putting her at ease. He'd fitted the mattress with silk sheets and strategically positioned candles throughout the room to provide sufficient, yet romantic light.

Hanging the floor to ceiling mirror had been a shitload of work, but dammit, the look in Cat's eyes as she perused the room had made it worthwhile.

Her gaze fell upon his padded workout bench that he'd

purposely positioned in front of the mirror. Her quick intake of breath hadn't gone unnoticed. He could almost hear that inquisitive mind of hers racing, wondering how he planned on using that particular prop.

Sam pulled a lighter from his pocket and lit the candles, creating an aura of warmth and coziness. Pushing her hair off her face, Cat stepped farther into the room. The light fell over her, bathing her body in a soft golden glow. The erotic vision bombarded his body with lust and need and something else, something just out of grasp, something he couldn't quite put a name to.

Something, he suspected, he was better off leaving nameless.

He crossed the room to stand before her. His movements were slow, deliberate, giving her time to absorb her surroundings, to get comfortable.

"Everything okay?" He shrugged his coat off and tossed it over a nearby chair.

She nodded. "Yes." Deft fingers began working the buttons on her coat. "The room looks beautiful. Not at all what I expected."

He grinned, pleased that she approved. A woman like Cat deserved only the best. "You were nice enough to volunteer your services. It's the least I could do to help you relax and make you comfortable."

"Still, you didn't have to go through so much trouble," she said, her voice a rough whisper. She removed her coat, placed it over his, and tipped her head. Sexual tension hung heavy in the air as he stood there basking in the glow of her sensuous body.

He stepped closer. Using the backs of his fingers, he caressed her cheek, surfing the outline of her jaw as he gazed into her eyes. She leaned into him, letting him know she welcomed his touch. He really loved her inhibition and her feminine confidence.

Contrary to what he'd told himself earlier that day, he had the distinct impression that Cat wasn't anything at all like the other women he'd had sex with.

Damned if that didn't scare the hell out of him.

Pressing her palms flat against his chest, she splayed her fingers, caressing and exploring his hard angles. The sweet friction penetrated his defenses. His stomach knotted like a pretzel.

"It wasn't any trouble. Beside, you're worth it," he said, knowing he meant every word of it. Her pretty pink tongue slid over her lips. Her sensuous mouth lifted in a half-smile. He watched, transfixed, as his gut rolled. A riot of foreign emotions took hold, leaving him feeling disorientated and perplexed.

Her grateful smile stirred something inside him. His

heart hammered. Edging closer, he breathed in her arousing feminine scent. Fuck, he wanted her. Fast and hard. Every fiber in his body demanded he touch her. To push inside her warm sheath. To feel her creamy essence drip over his cock as he claimed her. Branded her. Possessed her. He called on every ounce of strength and coached himself to control his primal urges and slow down, to make this good for her.

He angled his head and anchored her hips to his. It pleased him the way her body liquefied under his touch. Her lashes fluttered shut as their bodies melded. The silky sweep of her hair against his neck flooded him with lust, deepening his need. He feathered his lips over the hollow of her throat and could feel her pulse race.

He framed her face with his hands, stroking her cheek with his thumb. "You look beautiful tonight, Cat. I should have told you that earlier."

As though moving of their own volition, her legs widened, her eyes glazed with desire. He wedged his thigh in between hers. Heat radiated from her sex and it took all he had not to drop to the ground and press his mouth against her sweet spot. To inhale her, to taste her, to push his tongue all the way inside her hot core. To please her like she'd never been pleased before. He'd always taken the time to satisfy his women, but suddenly her pleasures were of the utmost importance. His old frat house mantra rushed through his mind. *When I'm on my knees I aim to please.*

"Thanks. You clean up pretty good yourself." Her voice hitched. Her seductive gaze panned the room and he wondered what she was thinking.

He stroked her cheek. "I want you to relax and enjoy this, Cat."

"I'm relaxed," she assured him. "And I'm ready," she paused and glanced at his bench, "for whatever you have in mind."

Chapter 3

Relaxed!

Oh yeah, she was relaxed alright. About as relaxed as a pen full of turkeys the day before Thanksgiving. Less than five hours ago she'd never expected to be locked inside a research room with six feet of drop-dead-gorgeous stimuli.

Did life get any better than this?

So what if he'd never paid any attention to her before. So what if she was simply his own personal lab rat, and once this experiment was over, things would go back to normal. Wasn't that what she wanted, anyway?

"Then let's begin. Come with me." Cat accepted his offered hand and let him guide her across the room until they stood before the mirror. To think this bad boy, this playboy, as Jen had referred to him, had gone through so much trouble to make the room perfect in a bid to relax her. He might act the Casanova, but deep down Cat caught glimpses of a true gentleman. She suspected there was much more to him than met the eye. His chivalry warmed her right down to her toes. And the way he took measures to assure her comfort proved Sam was a thoughtful, considerate guy.

The kind of guy she'd choose to settle down with and raise a family. If she ever wanted to settle down, that is. Which she didn't. She had to put all her energy and concentration into her career if she wanted to make it into the big league. A husband and kids didn't fit into that plan.

Pressing on her shoulder, he gently eased her down. "Have a seat."

With her gaze locked on his, Cat lowered herself onto the bench. She suddenly found herself presented with a full, un-obstructed view of his crotch. Ah, and what a lovely crotch it was. As her tongue darted between parched lips, she listened to the slight change in Sam's breathing as he scrutinized her every movement.

She lifted her eyes and met his penetrating stare. His ex-pression told her nothing. Maybe it was time to do a little experimenting of her own. Just because he had to test her responses didn't mean she couldn't test his. Maybe she could show him what he'd been missing all these months.

Sam dropped to his knees, gripped her legs and spread them.

Oh my!

Forget chivalry. Chivalry was overrated. She wanted him to throw her down caveman style and have his wicked way with her. Until sun up. Next week.

The girth of his broad shoulders pushed her wider as he insinuated himself in between. Her heart picked up pace. She caught the reflection of his perfect, sculpted ass in the mirror and hoped he couldn't see the drool pooling at the corners of her mouth.

Her eyes traveled back to his face. The soft glow from the candlelight made his skin glisten. Heat radiated from him as his blatant masculine scent curled her toes. White-hot desire claimed her, leaving her feeling a little dizzy, a little drugged.

With her pulse racing, it took all her effort to keep her voice steady, seductive. "Since I know my own body's responses better than anyone, maybe I should start by showing you what I like." She'd never pleasured herself in front of a man before, but then again she'd never been anyone's lab rat either. This guy brought out a completely different side of her.

Trying for sultry, she toyed with the top button on her blouse, tempting him. "What do you say?"

Sam's Adam's apple bobbed as he swallowed. His eyebrow rose a fraction, his gaze latched upon her breasts.

She leaned forward, her mouth a hairbreadth away from

his. His burning gaze moved to her face and settled on her parted lips.

His tongue traveled over his bottom lip, moistening, preparing. He slanted his mouth.

In that instant, Cat knew he was going to kiss her. Her pulse skyrocketed. Her body hummed with renewed excitement. For months she had fantasized about what his lips would feel like on hers. Now she was finally going to find out.

She dropped her voice to a whisper. "Unless you had something else in mind."

His eyes darkened, his tone deepened, his mouth curved enticingly. The air around them crackled with charged electricity.

"I like your idea, Cat." The fierce need and desire in his voice whipped through her like a powerful aphrodisiac. "I really do." He threaded his fingers through her hair. Tugging slightly, he drew her mouth to his. "And I like that you're comfortable enough to do that in front of me. But maybe I'd prefer to discover all your likes and all your secret desires on my own."

Well, who was she to voice an argument? After all, it was his experiment.

She moaned in acquiescence as he pressed his lips hungrily into hers. Heat licked over her body, moisture collected on her forehead. His tongue skated over her lips then sank inside for a slow exploration. She opened for him, granting him access, reveling in the feel of his velvet tongue mating with hers. Her body trembled, her nipples beaded and tightened to the point of pain, beckoning his touch, demanding his undivided attention. Urgent, unrelenting pressure brewed deep in her womb. A low erotic whimper bubbled in the depth of her dry throat.

Yes, perhaps his idea was better.

His tongue swept through her mouth like a firestorm, scorching her with his heat. He kissed her, long and hard, and with such passion it left her gulping for her very next breath.

Letting him know in no uncertain terms what she wanted, she tightened her legs and shifted forward, until their groins bumped. Her thighs hugged his hips, drawing him in closer, aching to feel him inside. A silent gesture that alerted him to the passion building in her body, threatening to burn her up from the inside out. As she gyrated against him, her aroused scent perfumed the air and closed in on them.

God, this was better than any fantasy she'd ever had.

For a long time, they traded kiss for kiss. Pleasure for pleasure. A low growl of satisfaction rumbled in his throat when he felt her responses. He inched back, his nostrils flared. A slow burn simmered in his eyes as he inhaled, filling his lungs with her feminine aroma. The intent look on his face made her pussy muscles quake.

She concentrated on the increasing ache and the sensations he invoked as his expert fingers idly stroked her thighs. He pressed his thumbs into her legs and climbed higher, until he closed in on her engorged clitoris. He stroked her through her jeans. Liquid heat pooled in her loins. She opened her mouth to gasp, but no sound came. In a silent plea, her body tensed, bowed into his touch.

Her tongue found the warmth of his mouth again and drew him in for a deep, mind-numbing kiss. Sam growled and pitched forward, pressing his erection harder against her. His breathing turned labored. He broke the kiss and licked his lips as though savoring the taste of her.

Urgent need colored his voice when he spoke. "Very sweet, Cat. Very, very sweet. I can't wait to discover if the rest of you is just as delicious."

Holy hell, neither could she.

The muscles in his jaw flexed and she sensed his restraint, sensed he was holding himself back. She could feel the wild feral passion mounting in him, rising higher and higher, threatening to consume them both. She suspected if he ever let go and gave himself completely over to his primal needs and unleashed his passion, his world would never be the same again.

And neither would hers.

His hands stroked her through her clothes, his corded muscles bunched with each torturous caress. "Are you ready to play, Cat?" His voice held a challenge that stole her speech-making capabilities.

Since a reply was beyond her, she simply shivered at the promise in his eyes.

"Are you ready for me to test your responses to my stimuli?" He breathed a kiss over her mouth.

Cat drew a shuddery breath, recovered her voice, and asked calmly, "How so?"

His low chuckle seeped into her skin, flooding her with warmth, drawing her far deeper into this game of seduction than she'd have thought possible.

"You're always so full of questions. Must be the journalist in you." God, his deep rasp did mysterious things to her insides.

His features softened as he sat back on his heels and tugged her blouse out from her waistband. His fingers connected with her skin, his gentle caress touching her so deeply she thought she'd die.

"Why don't you shut that inquisitive mind of yours off for a while and let me do my job." Tenderness in his voice tugged at her insides. He cupped her aching orbs through her blouse and kneaded, increasing the pressure deep between her legs. "Let me push you beyond your wildest imagination. Then tomorrow night, we'll see if we can go further."

* * *

Desire moved into Cat's stomach. Sensory overload drew a shudder from somewhere deep inside. If Sam pushed her any further, she feared she'd splinter into a million tiny fragments. Images of what the serum would do to her already sexually heightened libido sent equal measures of anxiety and excitement churning through her.

Candlelight flickered, casting seductive shadows on the walls as Sam climbed out from between her legs and circled behind her. She watched him in the mirror. He moved with such sexual confidence, a feminine thrill rushed through her and increased her pulse.

He threw a leg over the bench, lowered himself down, and shimmied forward, crowding her. Long muscular legs straddled her from behind, tightening around her hips, anchoring her in place. His hands spanned her waist, urging her closer. She could feel his desire and warmth reaching out to her. A strange, primal sound unlike anything she'd ever heard before crawled out of her throat.

"That's a girl." His voice and manner coaxed her to let go and do nothing but enjoy.

When she felt his cock indent the small of her back, she became pliable in his arms. Her mind stopped working, obviously his intention all along. Sam didn't want her to think; he only wanted her to feel. Exhaling, she closed her eyes, deciding to do just that.

The feel of his thick erection pressing into her flesh drew

her full attention. Some small coherent part of her brain alerted her to his rock-hard arousal.

This man that she'd wanted for so long wanted her too.

A rush of heat whipped through her blood. That same small coherent part also warned her to tread carefully. Warning her that Sam had the ability to seep under her skin in a way no other man ever had, and one night with him might cause her to want to be more than just his lab rat.

He pulled her hair from her shoulders, draping it over her back. His hands were gentle and soft against her flesh. The play of his fingers in her curls sent shivers of warm need to the depths of her soul. The way he pulled emotional reactions from her took her by surprise and threw her off balance.

He moaned against her throat then placed the sweetest, lightest kiss just below her earlobe. Her breath skidded to a halt. His lips were barely there, barely touching yet it did mysterious things to her nerve endings. He stroked her sensitive skin with his tongue, licking, laving until she nearly erupted all over him. Her body convulsed. She gulped air but still couldn't seem to fill her lungs.

She met his gaze in the mirror. His sexy grin turned lethal. "Mmmm. . . . Very nice, Cat. Very responsive." Lust darkened his eyes, his voice dripped with desire. "Just like I imagined you would be."

He cuffed her wrists and moved her hands to his thighs. "Keep your hands here," he commanded in a gentle voice.

The way he said it, the way his deep voice stirred all her emotions, sent a quiver along her spine. She held his glance in the mirror and forced a smile, hoping like hell he couldn't see into the depths of her soul, couldn't see the emotions churning inside her. Emotions she had no idea she'd feel.

As she studied his features, she tried not to melt all over him. Her heart did a little loop. The man simply did the strangest things to her insides.

His fingers moved to the front of her blouse. He played with the material and then lazily began to work open her buttons. Her lids fluttered. He popped one button, then another. Much too slowly for her liking. Engorged nipples pulsed in eager anticipation. She squirmed and shifted in her seat, suddenly very needy, very impatient for him to answer the pull deep between her trembling thighs.

"Sam."

His penetrating gaze locked on hers. "Hmmm?" he whispered with dark seduction.

He eased open her shirt, pulled it from her shoulders, and let it pool around her back. She caught her own reflection in the mirror and barely recognized the woman staring back. Hair swimming in disarray around her shoulders, her face was colored from heat and desire.

She arched against him, breathless. Waiting was no longer an option. "Would you please hurry?" Her voice ended in an agonized whisper.

His low chuckle wrapped around her. "I'll see what I can do." He cupped her breasts, hugging them with his palms. He pulled them high as his thumbs slipped inside her red silky bra to manipulate her tight nipples.

Her blood pressure soared. "Oh God, Sam. That feels wonderful."

She listened to him swallow. "Oh yeah, it sure does." He leaned forward and unhooked the front clasp. His hair brushed her nape, teasing her senses.

Like air seeping from a punctured tire, Sam let out a slow, wheezing breath as he freed her swollen breasts from the restrictive confines. Discarding the flimsy material, he stroked her naked skin, caressing the swell of her cleavage, brushing his fingers in a circular motion around her pale mounds, drawing closer and closer to the coveted peaks.

Her lids slipped shut against the gentle assault. Tension coiled deep inside her. "Sam . . . please." Sheer desperation for him to take her now, fast and hard, made her whimper. She'd never been so deeply aroused, so desperate, so needy.

The responses this man pulled from her were unlike any-thing she'd ever felt before.

She'd had good sex before, not great sex, but good sex all the same. Men had seduced her body, but none had ever taken the time to seduce all her senses. The combination brought her to this foreign place, a place where an incessant ache and burn made her shamelessly cry out for release. A place where Sam touched her on a completely different level.

A moment later he found her beaded nipples and began rolling them between his thumb and fingers. Pinching, squeezing, and pulling. Just when she thought she couldn't take anymore, he'd push her further beyond her boundaries. Then, giving her reprieve, he'd switch tactics, caressing her softly, gently, easing the throbbing ache. The mixture of pain and pleasure was most exquisite.

"Your breasts are beautiful." For a brief moment she thought she saw a flash of possessiveness in his eyes. Surely she was mistaken. "Have you ever orgasmed from a man touching your nipples, Cat?"

His rich baritone sent a barrage of erotic sensations straight to her damp pussy. Her sex muscles began to shudder and clench. She rocked in her seat, pushing her hooded clitoris against the seam of her jeans, searching for some kind of release, something to help quell the unbearable ache. God, she'd never felt so crazed, so frantic.

"No," she moaned as passion exploded through her. He smiled and she wondered why that pleased him. Did he want to be the first to try? The first to succeed? Did that matter to him somehow?

He dusted kisses over her neck and whispered in the softest sexiest voice, "Then it's time you did."

She gasped. Lord, there she went, gasping again. Man, she really needed to work on that.

"And I'm just the man to do it."

Her hands tightened on his thighs, nails digging into his flesh. She swallowed, wanting to believe it possible, but knowing her body didn't work that way. Not unless Sam was some kind of miracle worker.

She looked heavenward. *Please let Sam be a miracle worker.*

"I don't think I can, Sam."

"Well see about that." The fierce determination in his voice made her mouth go dry. She arched into him, hot and wanting. Wet anticipation dampened her panties.

Her hand slipped off his thighs and nestled between her legs. Desperate for pleasure, she gave herself a light stroke, in an effort to ease the tension. Unfortunately, the friction only aroused her more. She moaned and rubbed her thumb over her aching clit.

Sam caught her action in the mirror. "Dammit, Cat." She heard the clench of his teeth and the lusty groan low in his throat. Without warning he caught hold of her wrist and stopped her. Cat sensed he was on the edge, and pleasuring herself would ultimately send him hurtling over.

"Put it back," he ordered, sharply. "Tonight it's my job to touch you."

With excruciating slowness, he trailed his fingers over her flesh, his teeth scraping over her neck, his lips pressing hot kisses against her skin. Sensations closed in on her as he stroked her with expertise. She squeezed her lids and moaned, almost delirious with want.

"Open your eyes, Cat. I need to see your responses." His voice was low, coaxing, demanding.

She rested her head against his shoulder, clenched her fingers around his hard thigh muscles, and struggled to find her voice. Her lips caught between her teeth, her breath shuddered.

"I can't, Sam. It's too intense."

He pressed his lips close to her ear, close to that erogenous zone that made her tremble like a wanton woman. His heated breath scorched her skin as he spoke. Her body responded with a shudder.

"Yes you can, babe. Do it for me."

Her lids fluttered open. Her glance collided with his. The dark desire she met in his eyes completely unglued her. Her heavy breasts, encased in his warm hands, filled with heated blood.

She'd never come from nipple stimulation before, but the seductive room, the expert ministrations of his hands, and the emotions Sam pulled from her raised her passion to new heights.

Sam drew his finger to his mouth, licked it, and placed it

over her nipple. Her whole body went up in flames. The wet, hot sensation pushed her to the edge of sanity. Oh God! She bit down on her lip and flushed darker. Sam touched her so deeply she feared she'd never be the same after this night.

"Ahh, I see you like that. Let me see what else you like. What other responses I can pull from you."

He applied more pressure to her sensitive nerve endings, determined to make her soak her panties right then and there. She moaned and arched into his touch, deciding that was a damn good idea.

He began panting heavily in response to her blatant need. Their aroused scents mingled. His breath became hotter and faster against the column of her neck. His sheer excitement pushed her passion impossibly higher.

He inched back, leaving cold where there was once heat. Her hands slid off his thighs and fell to her sides. "No, don't stop, Sam. *Please . . .*" Lord, she'd never heard such desperation in her voice before. She began to shake and vibrate with sexual frustration.

She heard a soft chuckle, but she didn't particularly find his sexual torture amusing.

With slow, confident moves, he stood and circled around to face her hard-on . . . err . . . straight on. His eyes dropped to her swollen, achy, exposed breasts. Promise glittered in his piercing blue eyes.

"I'm just getting started, Cat."

Oh, good.

Dark, prominent nipples quivered under his hungry gaze. She cupped her orbs in offering as if to say, "Then get started." His growl filled her with raw lust.

Pushing gently on her shoulders, he lowered her on the bench until she found herself flat on her back. Oh hell, he'd hung a mirror on the ceiling too. Her throat closed over. Had he somehow tapped into one of her nightly fantasies?

Sam sat facing her and drew her legs up until they rested over his. Uncomfortable in her damp panties, she shimmied her backside, aching for him to remove them. His eyes fixed on her swaying breasts. God, she really was a wanton woman.

His lips twitched. "Soon, Cat. I promise."

She'd never met anyone so in tune with her needs or desires. Her heart did another little dance, more like hip-hop this time.

Gaze riveted, he took a long moment, just staring at her breasts in obvious admiration. Passion clouded his eyes. God, the way he looked at her made her feel like the sexiest woman alive.

Sam leaned forward and swiped his hot, velvet tongue across her hard nipples, moistening her flesh. Ever so lightly he blew, tightening her pebbled nubs in painful bliss with the hot, cold medley. Her skin warmed from head to toe and came alive at the evocative sensations.

"Oh, Sam," she whispered, teetering on the edge. "I can't believe how close I am." Her pussy muscles undulated with each delicious stroke. Before today she never would have believed that she'd ever climax from nipple stimulation. In truth, few men were skilled enough to master such a feat.

Suddenly, Jen's words came back to haunt her, reminding her of Sam's numerous indiscretions and his exceptional talent in the bedroom. Her stomach churned. She swallowed and reminded herself it didn't matter.

Sam growled and brought his mouth close to hers. "Cat, you are so damn responsive it's making me throb."

She threaded her fingers through his hair and guided his head down, back to her mounds, encouraging him to lick and suck and nibble until she died from too much pleasure. It'd be a good way to die, she decided.

There was a note of desperation in her voice. Her eyes pleaded. "More, Sam. Please."

He smiled in reaction to her plea then dipped his head to answer her urgent demands. Slowly, methodically, giving her breasts undivided attention, he caressed her nipples with his tongue. Her heart nearly failed. She writhed and moaned beneath his ravishing mouth.

Cat couldn't believe how erotic it was to watch the action in the mirror. Nor could she believe how aroused he'd made her. She began trembling with urgency as the need for him to ease the tension between her thighs completely consumed her. She'd never felt so frantic, so out of control.

He pulled his mouth away and paid homage to her other nipple. Treating it to the same erotic tongue bath, pushing her beyond all her limits, making her wild. Wilder than she'd ever been before.

Panting with utter excitement, she could barely find her breath as he manipulated her breasts. Her stomach knotted; her throat dried. His mouth branded her, searing her quaking flesh with his heat. Every nerve ending in her body vibrated and quaked. She tossed her head from side to side, a fever dampening her forehead.

He deepened the kiss. Sparks shot through her body. Sharp teeth nipped, nibbled, and toyed with her swollen pebbles, his tongue soothing the sting left behind. A lethal combination that proved too intense for her to bear. Pain and pleasure gripped her. Her stomach clenched.

"Sam stop, it's too much." She reached for his shoulders to push him off, but he shackled her hands and pinned them above her head.

He made a sexy noise and shifted. His eyes ravished her with dark hunger. "Let go, Cat. Let me take you where you need to go." The soft coaxing tone of his voice seeped into her skin and assailed her already overstimulated senses. As his mouth closed over her flesh again, her orgasm took her by surprise. Suddenly, she felt that first sweet, all-consuming clench of total and utter fulfillment. She drew a breath, letting Sam take her to a place where nothing mattered but pleasure.

His tongue swirled around her engorged nipple, keeping up its gentle assault, adding fuel to the raging fire inside her.

She whimpered. "That feels incredible," she whispered.

"And it tastes incredible," Sam said between each determined swipe.

She took deep, gulping breaths and let herself topple over. Tumultuous emotions charged through her as liquid heat surged from her pussy with more intensity than she'd ever felt before.

Her whole body tensed, then relaxed. "Sam, I'm coming," she cried out, certain that he already knew, but deciding to tell him just the same.

"Look at yourself in the mirror, babe. Watch yourself come while I watch you," he whispered.

She watched her body writhe as she gave herself over to her orgasm. The room closed in on her as she focused completely on the stab of pleasure at the apex of her legs. She threw her head back and lifted her hips from the bench as her climax tore through her. Her mind blanked to everything around her except the intense pleasure of Sam's mouth on her breasts and the pulsing between her thighs.

Still licking her nipples with long, luxurious strokes, Sam held her to him, balancing her until her world turned right side up again. After a comfortable stretch of silence, her labored breathing finally settled into a calmer, steadier rhythm.

His dark eyes met hers as he pulled her to him. She sat up, her breasts crushed against a wall of thick muscle. Damp curls fell over her forehead.

Eyes full of want, Sam shot her a tender look of intimacy that made her heart tighten. She shivered, almost violently. The way he gazed at her drew her in to a cocoon of warmth. She felt so close to him. She touched his face, needing the contact. Her throat clogged. Her insides turned to mush. Leaning in, she pressed a soft kiss to his cheek. When her lashes fluttered against his skin, he shuddered.

She opened her mouth, not sure what she was about to say, not sure what she was about to reveal. He smiled and her heart did a somersault. God, she couldn't fall for him, she just couldn't. It would complicate everything. "Sam, I . . ." Her voice broke off.

He chuckled easily and lowered his voice to match hers. "I know." He brushed the rough pad of his thumb over her engorged nipple. "You never expected to orgasm from this kind of stimulation." He tucked her hair behind her ear. "You were pretty amazing, Cat. Very responsive to my touch. I really like that."

Her voice wasn't quite steady. "It's because you knew just how to touch me," she whispered with effort.

And everyone else, apparently.

She looked down, suddenly feeling very naked, very exposed. Very vulnerable. Very worried that she'd given herself to him in a way she'd never given herself to another. Her physical need for him may have been temporarily sated, but her emotional need for him was reaching dangerous levels.

Trying for casual she said, "So I guess that concludes your experiment until tomorrow night." God, she hated the way her voice cracked.

Sam angled his head. "Tell me, Cat. Do you have any other plans for tonight?"

"Why?"

The way he looked at her made her shiver. "Because," he touched her chin and dragged his finger over her neck. "If you do, I want you to break them."

"You do. Why?" Her heart hammered with what felt like hope. God, she wanted him again. Inside out, upside down, but mostly on underneath.

He spoke in whispered words. "Because I'm not nearly done with you."

Her chin jerked up. Her eyes widened. "Really? There's more?" She didn't even make an attempt to hide her enthusiasm. What would be the point? It seemed Sam could read her every gesture, her every hidden desire.

He stroked his thumb over her mouth and then replaced his fingers with his lips, lightly feathering them over hers. She opened for him as the sensations fueled her need for him all over again.

Sam gave her a playful look and whispered into her mouth, "Plenty more, Cat. We're just getting started." His voice, full of tender warmth, drew a shudder from the depths of her soul.

Her heart stuttered; her breathing grew shallow. Perhaps offering herself in exchange had been a stupid idea, after all. If she spent another moment in his arms, she might end up wanting something deeper.

She forced herself to pull back emotionally. "Sam, I don't think I can take more." Her voice turned choppy, her words fractured. It occurred to her that Sam's brand of lovemaking would tip the emotional scales to the point of no return.

His wicked grin made her weak. There was a note of amusement in his voice. "That's what we're going to find out."

Chapter *4*

Sam gripped her hips and lifted her from the bench. Curly blonde hair cascaded over her bare shoulders and slid down her perfect round breasts. Her eyes were drowsy, sated. Desire slammed him into outfield. He felt like he'd received a blow to the midsection.

God, he loved the way she gave herself over to him so freely, so completely. And knowing he was the first man to bring her to orgasm through nipple stimulation thrilled him, probably far more than it should have.

As he gazed at her a moment longer, a wave of possessiveness tore through him. His body ached to join with hers, to lose himself in the heat between her legs. It took all his effort not to tear his clothes off, sink his cock into her plush softness and ravish her all night long.

Of course, he had every intention of doing just that, right

after he tasted her sweetness and drew another orgasm from her, using his mouth and his fingers. His whole body broke a sweat in anticipation. Moisture sealed his shirt to his chest. He brushed his damp hair from his forehead and sucked in a fortifying breath.

As Cat stood, her legs wobbled. She snaked her arms around his shoulders, steadying herself.

"Easy," he said, tightening his hold. "Are you able to stand?"

She nodded, her body melting against his, her nipples hard against his chest, battering what little control he had left.

"Good, because what I have in mind requires you to be upright." He felt her body quake with yearning, her eyes growing wide at the promise in his voice.

It touched him and stirred something deep inside the way she shivered with longing for him. In fact, a lot of things about Cat Nichols touched him, making it harder and harder to separate sex and emotion.

Banking his muddled feelings, Sam stood behind her. With his chest molded against her back, he linked his fingers through hers. "Walk with me."

Steps synchronized, he urged her toward the mirror. Her gorgeous, swollen breasts swayed with each seductive movement. Sam growled and pressed his thick, steel erection harder between the soft mounds of her ass.

Cat drew a quick breath and wiggled her curvy hips. Sam growled louder, his cock throbbing against her sweet backside.

"I'm not the only one who is very responsive," Cat said.

He caught the teasing glint in her eyes.

"If you keep that up, we won't be testing your responses; we'll be testing my limits."

Sam lifted her arms above her head and pressed her flat palms to the mirror. He caught her glance. Green eyes narrowed with dark seduction and bore into his. She widened her stance and her expression turned serious. "Maybe that's what I have in mind," she said, her voice rough with emotion.

The sexual energy between them exploded, reaching an all time high. His body reacted to the desire in her eyes. His blood began racing. His heart slammed against his chest. Wild, untamed passion stirred inside him, boiling, rising, gaining raw energy, drawing his full attention. He gripped her hips, tipping her ass up, and pushed his pulsing cock hard against her lush backside. It didn't even begin to ease the ache. The only thing that would help assuage the hot restlessness in his groin was to feel her naked skin against his.

Shoulders forward, she inched her feet back. With her ass tucked against his groin she smothered his erection and gyrated. The position proved his undoing.

"I want you, Sam," she whimpered, spreading her legs even wider. "I want you inside me." She begged for him to take her, opening herself up, granting him access to her body.

He responded to the erotic pose and seductive lilt in her voice. Fingers moving swiftly, he ripped open her jeans, lowered the zipper, and tugged them down her legs. Her panties quickly followed. She removed her shoes and kicked away her clothes. He took in the vision before him. The sight of her sensuous body on display with her hands braced against the mirror was enough to shred his last fragments of control.

With intense concentration, she followed his actions in the mirror as he tore his clothes off and tossed them into the heap with hers.

What was it about this sexy, feisty woman that turned him inside out? He'd never felt anything like it. The need, the passion, the desire welling up inside him. It curled around him, calling, consuming, reaching dangerous levels. He tried to leash his control, his passion, and his emotions, but failed miserably.

He had to have her.

Now.

Sam had never lost control before. Ever. But he'd never been taken to a place where the fierce need to possess another dominated his every thought.

His voice was labored. "Your shoes, Cat."

Heavy lids fluttered. "What about them?" She angled her head to see him.

"Put them back on."

Grinning, she quickly obliged. The high heels stretched out her long legs, lifting her ass in the air.

Pushing his raging erection against her naked flesh, he tangled his fingers through her sopping silk curls and buried his face against her throat. Her damp arousal made his legs tremble. He pulled open her pretty pink lips and exposed her sex in the mirror. With a long, lazy stroke he caressed her quivering clitoris. Her mouth formed an "O" when his fingers connected with her delicate pearl. She tossed her head to the side and moaned. Her body jerked against his pulsing cock and he nearly released on impact. He clenched his jaw and held back, never wanting the night to end.

He stretched her wider. His mouth salivated, eager for a taste. He slipped a finger all the way inside her moist fissure, stirring, caressing her G-spot, reveling in the feel of her plush softness.

Her tongue slid over her lips as though she knew his intentions. Their aroused scents merged and filled the room with a heady, stimulating aroma.

He applied more pressure to her sex. Using slow, sinuous circles, he teased her clit until it swelled and puckered beneath the rough pad of his fingers.

"Oh Sam," she cried, bucking against his hand. Color bloomed high on her cheeks. He watched her chest rise and fall in an erratic pattern. Her pussy muscles gripped his finger and he knew an orgasm was only a stroke away.

He inhaled her warm, familiar scent as it perfumed the air. Easing his finger out of her, he drew it to his mouth for a sampling.

"Sweet Jesus, you taste incredible." His voice was gruff with need.

She swallowed. "Sam. . . . Please . . . my purse . . . condoms."

He could barely hear her through the buzz in his head. He swept aside a lock of her hair, pressed his mouth against her ear, and caressed her cheek. She twisted her head and drew his finger into her mouth, sucking, licking, savoring her creamy essence.

The heat of her mouth nearly caused him to explode on the spot. He wanted to feast on her, to sear her engorged clitoris with his tongue, but that would have to wait. Right now he needed to answer the demands that threatened to burn them both up from the inside out.

His rock-hard erection throbbed to the point of pain. Cat dropped one hand, reached behind her, and squeezed his steel shaft, running her fingers up and down the length of him, driving him into an abyss of pleasure.

Heat and passion blazed through him. The intensity of

his carnal hunger was almost frightening. "Oh God. Cat. I need you."

Her voice was husky and breathless. "My purse. By the door. And please, hurry."

Her words drove him beyond the brink of sanity, making his cock drip. He brushed the wet tip of his arousal over her flesh. His liquid juice dripped over her back, languidly sliding lower to nestle between the sweet slit of her heart-shaped ass.

Christ, that turned him on.

He disentangled himself and grabbed her purse. He had his own supply of condoms in the nightstand, but decided, in his haste to sheathe himself, her purse was closer. He ripped open the condom and slid it on. When he turned back around to face Cat, what he saw nearly dropped him to his knees. His body tightened and his vision went fuzzy around the edges as unfamiliar warmth touched the depths of his soul.

Hand between her legs, she stroked her clitoris, sliding her slender finger in and out of her heated core. Long hair fell forward, curling around her pert nipples. Candlelight bathed her naked body and glistened on her moist pussy.

Sweat collected on his brow. He drew a shaky breath. "Sweet fuck, Cat." In two quick strides he crossed the room. He put his mouth close to her ear and murmured, "Need a hand." Without waiting for a response, he placed his finger over hers, pushing both his and her finger deep inside her at the same time. Cat panted, moaned, and shook as another orgasm ripped through her.

Lord, he'd never met a more responsive woman. His cock jerked, clamoring for attention. Sam grabbed her hips and positioned his erection at her dripping entrance.

"Look at me," he growled.

Cat tilted her head and met his gaze in the mirror. It was easy to tell she was overcome with need by the passion raging in her eyes. She inched back, until his cock probed her, opening her feminine folds. Her tight heat and rich female texture beckoned him. Sexual tension swamped them. Completely ruled by lust, his mind abandoned any rational thought.

His growl deepened. "Cat, you feel so good." In one quick thrust he speared her.

"Oh . . . my," she whispered as he drove into her.

She shifted her stance, the position allowing her to take the entire length of his shaft. Cat gasped and stilled as he pushed impossibly deeper, stretching open the tight walls of her pussy.

He felt her heat close around him, squeezing. His eyes locked with hers. "Cat, I need to take you. Now," he bit out between clenched teeth. He couldn't wait for her to catch up. He tried, he really did, but that small modicum of control and distance he'd always kept during sex jumped ship and left him frenzied, wide open, and vulnerable. For the first time ever, his guard slipped and he let go. Really let go.

"Then take me, Sam."

His internal temperature soared. He needed her so much he felt dizzy. Hard and fast he began pumping, pounding against her feminine mound. She met his every thrust with one of her own. The warmth of her slick sheath made him sweat. He leaned forward and cupped her breasts, his fingers kneading her swollen pebbles. With his chest pressed against her back, their perspiration mingled, their deep breaths merged, fogging the mirror. Heat poured from his body to hers and back again.

They joined as one with Sam controlling the pace, depth, and rhythm. He clenched his jaw, trying to hold off his orgasm. His mind began spinning. His thoughts scattered. He wanted to stay inside her, to revel in her passion-drenched heat. To claim her, to possess her, to have her climb inside him and stay there forever so he didn't ever have to share her with another man. Unfamiliar emotions rushed through him. His gut rolled. His pulse kicked up a notch. Air rushed from his lungs. Fuck, some small part of his mind reminded him that he'd never been so crazed before, so frantic, and had never lost control.

Ever.

Oh hell.

He felt her pussy tighten around his cock. She bucked and impaled herself on him.

Her head thrashed to the side. *"Sam . . ."*

Hands biting into her hips, he buried himself deep as her orgasm rolled through her.

"Cat . . ."

Her liquid heat seared his cock, pushing the right buttons, sending him all the way to heaven and back again.

With one hard thrust he drove into her and stilled, concentrating on the points of pleasure as his climax mounted. His cock clenched and throbbed. His seed spurted from his tip.

"Oh God, Cat . . ." he whispered into her ear as his orgasm tore through him. As he emptied himself into her, he felt her sex muscles tighten, milking him of every drop.

He stayed there for a long moment, working to regulate his breathing while his cock grew flaccid. Minutes later he slipped from her opening. Cat twisted around, glanced into his eyes, and broke the stretch of silence.

She ran her tongue over her bottom lip, moistening it. "Sam." The warmth of her mouth called out to him.

"Yeah?" He quickly discarded the condom and then took her back in his arms, unable to get her close enough.

She tilted her chin to face him and pressed her back against the mirror. Hands spanning her slim waist, he gathered her in tighter, needing to feel every inch of her pressed against him, knowing he'd never felt such an easy intimacy with another.

Oh boy!

Unwelcome images of those six different men parading in and out of her condo rushed through his mind and filled him with rage. Like the Loch Ness Monster, anger rose from the depths to rear its ugly head.

The way he reacted with such violence gave him concern. Wasn't that one of the reasons Cat had appealed to him? She was safe. Not looking for anything more than he could give.

Tamping down his anger and cursing himself for feeling so emotional, he forced himself to marshal his thoughts and summon control.

Cat smiled up at him and moistened her dry lips. "That was one hell of an experiment, Sam." Eyes full of want flashed in the candlelight, her sweet breath fanned his face, closing around him, flooding him with longing.

He chuckled, smoothed her hair from her forehead, and crushed his body against hers. As she snuggled into him, a rush of tenderness made his stomach roll.

"I'll say," he managed around the lump forming in his throat.

He inched back his gaze roaming her face. When their eyes met, desire slammed into him once more, triggering a craving that he couldn't sate. His cock stirred back to life. What was it about this woman? Why couldn't he get enough of her?

Sam let out a regretful sigh. "Only one problem."

Her sexy brow rose. Heavy breasts swayed, dragging his eyes with them. "Problem?"

He gripped her hands, pinning them behind her back. Her slick body molded against his and all he could think about was dropping to the ground, parting her twin lips with his tongue, and pressing a kiss over her gorgeous pink sex. "Yeah. You see, I was so caught up in fucking you I forgot to record your responses."

She swiped her tongue over her bottom lip, made a sexy noise, and rotated her hips. Their groins bumped. Sam's cock thickened. His balls constricted.

"That's not good, Sam."

"Nope, not good at all."

"What does that mean?" He loved the teasing lilt in her voice. Loved this playful side of her and her adventurous spirit. Once again, the hunger inside him took hold, consuming his thoughts.

He frowned. "I'm afraid I'm going to have to run the experiment again."

She took a moment to digest what he said, then shook her head in mock exasperation. Her soft whisper covered him.

"Where are you ever going to find another lab rat this time of night?" Suddenly her eyes opened wide. "There is always Bonnie," she rushed out.

Sam chuckled at the mention of his lab rat. "Can't."

"No?"

"Sleeping."

"Can't wake her?"

"Grumpy without her nine hours."

"I see."

"That really only leaves one solution."

"Only one?"

He crushed his body against hers and pushed his full fledged hard-on against her hip. "Only one," he said firmly, sending her a silent message, hoping to make her as crazy as she was making him.

She blew out an exaggerated breath. "Well hell, the things I have to do in the name of science."

Chapter 5

Sam shaded the early morning sun from his eyes as he tapped the brakes on his Jeep and rounded the corner to the Research Center. Stifling a yawn, he angled his head, anxious to see if the huge mob picketing the front entrance had dwindled any since yesterday.

Chances were, if the crowd had dissipated, normal testing would once again resume, which meant he'd no longer need Cat's assistance. That thought settled in his stomach like a lump of cold oatmeal. The problem was, even after last night's delicious experiment, he hadn't quite finished with the little wildcat yet or gotten her out of his system.

There was something different, something intriguing about Cat that made him want to keep her around longer. Maybe it was the way she cared about his future and stepped up to help him when he needed it. No woman had ever really cared about him before. Not even his own mother or one of her stand-ins over the years, and certainly not any of the women he dated.

Or maybe it was the way Cat lacked inhibition around him, opening up and trusting him enough to give herself over to him completely last night, which in turn made him open up and give himself over to her.

A wave of unease curled around him, leaving him feeling a little off balance. He suspected this was a dangerous game they were playing. One that could ultimately end with him wanting more than a few nights of experimental sex.

Lessons learned early on reminded him to keep a modicum of distance. So what the hell happened to that modicum of distance when he'd sank into Cat's plush softness last night? Twice?

He worked to redirect his thoughts, forcing his mind not to conjure up heated memories of the way her plump lips parted and green eyes lit up while he brought her to orgasm. Over and over again. Tried not to think about the way his engorged cock felt inside her tight sheath as he too reached an earth-shattering climax. Twice.

Striving for nonchalance about what they'd done the previous night and what they were going to do again tonight, he took the corner to the back lot and shot a glance at the front entrance. A relieved rush of air exploded from his lungs when he spotted a few lone protestors milling about. He paused to consider his reactions.

He actually blew out a relieved breath . . . *fuck*.

Less than twenty-four hours ago, he'd been kick-ass mad about all the negative attention and the fall out from Cat's article. Now, here he was, fucking happy to see the protestors back.

Happy, for Christ sake.

He had to be insane. Or perhaps he'd sniffed one too many chemicals at the lab. That had to be the only logical explanation.

Sam parked in the underground parkade, tossed his backpack over his shoulder, and entered the building through the rear entrance, avoiding the last of the die-hard protestors.

He climbed the stairs and started toward the front security counter. After he signed in, he made his way to the elevator. He spotted Kale coming from the stairwell.

With a hurried gait, Kale rushed to catch up. "Hey, Sam."

"How's it going?" Sam asked, noting the weary lines around Kale's eyes. "Another rough night?"

Kale smiled. "It shows?"

Sam jabbed the elevator button. "Why don't you drop Samantha off with me some night this week so you and Erin can get some rest?"

Kale clapped Sam's shoulders. "Now there's an offer I can't refuse." Kale yawned and stretched. "How about this weekend? There is a new movie opening Saturday we'd like to see. Erin and I can catch the matinee and then go to sleep right after dinner."

Sam chuckled. "Sounds great."

Kale arched a brow. "Unless babysitting on the weekend will interfere with your personal life. We could always wait until some day next week."

Sam shook his head. "No, it's not a problem."

"No big date this Saturday?" Kale probed.

Sam gave another quick shake and redirected the conversation. He had no intentions of discussing his personal life with Kale. "Why are you here anyway? You're off on leave for the next month. You should be home catching up on your sleep."

Concern etched Kale's face. "Because I wanted to talk to you." They both stepped onto the elevator.

Slanting his head, Sam met Kale's somber glance. Sam recognized that look. He'd encountered the serious side of Kale a time or two in the past, last night at his apartment being the most recent.

Sam starched his spine, his shoulders stiffening. "What's up?" he asked, suspecting he already knew the answer to that question.

Kale got right to the point. "I didn't realize it was the re-porter you had a *date* with."

Sam rolled one shoulder, looking casual, yet feeling any-thing but.

Kale cast him a knowing look. "She's a reporter, Sam. You need to start thinking with the right head."

Sam drove his hands deep into his pockets and fixed Kale with a look that told him to drop it. "I've got everything under control," he assured him.

Refusing to let it go, Kale crossed his arms, leaned against the wall and pressed on. "This is a dangerous game you're playing."

He didn't know the half of it.

When Sam didn't respond, Kale continued. "How do you know she's not trying to get close to you just to get another story?"

It wasn't like he hadn't thought of that himself. The truth was he really didn't know Cat very well at all. And damned if he didn't want to rectify that.

"She's a reporter, Sam. She can't be trusted."

She's also a woman. One who stepped in to aid him with his experiment, to help make things right for him after her article threatened his future. One who pulled far too many emotions from him. *Damn.*

He suddenly felt very protective of her. The same way he

felt protective of all those he cared about. He clenched his jaw and bit out, "Drop it, Kale."

"I only have your best interests at heart."

The elevator came to a grinding halt and the doors cleared.

"Be careful, Sam."

With Kale's words of warning echoing in his head, Sam stepped off and made his way down the hall.

He fisted his hands, annoyed, not only with Kale but with himself. Something about Cat had him acting completely out of character. He wasn't inclined to take risks with his work or the Research Center's security.

Sam knew Cat's drive and ambition matched his. That much was evident. And wouldn't Sam do anything to complete an assignment? Even go against protocol? What about Cat? How far would she go to get what she wanted?

Unnerved by the direction of his thoughts, Sam stopped outside his lab. He slipped his card through the electronic lock and pushed it open with much more force than necessary. He was immediately greeted by his wide awake and active chimp.

His mood lightened. "Hey Rio, how's it going girl?" He opened her cage and swung her to his hip. He signed, "Are you hungry?"

"Starving" was her answer. Sam chuckled, opened his backpack, and prepared Rio's breakfast. Once Rio had been taken care of, Sam turned his attention to the teetering stack of papers on his desk.

He blew out an exasperated breath and sank into his chair. He hated this part of the job. He'd rather be cooking up a new serum . . . or *testing said serum.*

His assistant usually filled out all the forms and reports, but with her grandmother's recent death, she'd been away from the lab for the past week.

Knowing the paperwork wasn't about to take care of itself, Sam dug in, his attention focused on the presentation he'd give the Grant Governing Board once his testing was complete. If all went according to plan, he'd be presenting his findings next week and securing future grants for the center. He'd yet to figure out how to explain it to his Director, but he was hoping once the grant came through, Reginald would let him off with a warning. At least he hoped so.

Elbow deep in filling out reports and documenting his findings to date, the morning flew by. Before he knew it his stomach began to grumble. He'd packed a sandwich in his backpack, but Sam knew that wouldn't sate his hunger. At that particular moment he had a craving for something else. And that something else was a vine-ripened, succulent orange.

Sam climbed from his chair and stretched. Maybe he'd shoot on over to the market and pick up a dozen oranges. As he threw his coat on and made his way to his door, a stack of mail caught his attention. Damn, it had been piling up for the last week. He picked it up and thumbed through it, stopping on the one and only envelope addressed directly to him.

He tore into it. His heart kicked into gear as he scanned the words. *Shit.* This was much more serious than he thought.

"Rio, come here." Rio dropped the blocks she'd been playing with, and with Sam's assistance, settled herself onto his hip.

As Sam read the note a second time, he pulled Rio in tighter. His anger flared and burned through him, his heart beat in a mad cadence. "Son of a bitch," he whispered under his breath. No one threatened those he cared about and got away with it.

He rushed from the lab and made his way to the Director's office. He found Reginald's door ajar. Sam knocked and poked his head in.

"I need to talk to you," Sam said.

Reginald waved him in. "Come in. I was just about to stop in to see you to discuss your research."

Sam's blood went cold. Shit. Had Reginald found out what he'd done last night? If so, they'd have to discuss it later. Right now he had more important things on his mind. Saving his ass would have to wait. Sam didn't give the Director a chance to elaborate.

Without waiting for an opening, he rushed on. "I think

we need to discuss this first." After adjusting Rio on his hip, he handed Reginald the note. Agitated, Sam fisted his hands and explained, "Some son of a bitch out there," he jerked his thumb toward the window, "threatened to kidnap Rio to keep her safe from my experiment. Jesus, what's it going to take to get it through to them that Rio is my pet?"

Reginald frowned as he scanned the words. He twisted in his chair, the seat groaning under his weight. "Well this really puts a crimp into things." He reached for the phone. "Time to contact Detective Doyle, I believe."

Pacing, Sam listened as Reginald discussed the situation with Detective Doyle. He remembered him from a few years back when the lab had been broken into by their competitors. After Reginald relayed the information, he hung up and turned his attention to Sam.

"They're on their way. I'll handle it." Reginald stood and walked over to his window. "Until they get to the bottom of this, I'd suggest you keep your eye on Rio and watch your back. Some of these protestors can get downright violent."

Sam's nostrils flared. "We'll see about that."

Reginald put his hand on Sam's shoulder, a calming gesture. "Listen," the Director said firmly, his voice laced with warning as though he read Sam's intentions. "Don't go out there. Let the police handle it. Lock Rio up in your lab, go get some fresh air, and cool off."

Sam exhaled a resigned breath, knowing he needed to blow

off some steam before he exploded and accosted a group of protestor's. Not a great move to help his cause.

Heeding the Director's advice, Sam secured Rio in her cage, took the elevator to the main lobby, and made his way to the underground parkade.

His mind raced with the unpleasant turn of events. He knew Rio would be safe at the lab, but what the hell would it take to get protestors off his back for Christ sake? He paused, giving it further thought. Perhaps another article by Cat would make a difference. Nothing had worked so far. Not even the news conference Reginald had held. Maybe asking her to write another piece was worth a shot. Nothing ventured, nothing gained, as they say. After all, a second article redeeming him and his experiment couldn't do any more harm.

Could it?

Sam maneuvered his Jeep into lunchtime traffic, taking a sharp left turn toward Cat's newspaper office. As he negotiated through the noon hour rush, he worked to convince himself that the threatening letter was the driving force behind his fierce need to see her. Not because the minute he'd dropped her off last night, he'd longed to feel her in his arms again and couldn't wait until tonight to see her.

Fuck. . .

* * *

Pleasure Exchange

Third cup of coffee in hand, Cat sipped and stared at the blank computer screen, willing the caffeine to take hold and clear the fog from her lust-saturated mind long enough for her to write something creative. At this particular moment, she'd even settle for something decipherable. Unfortunately she found herself too preoccupied with last night's delicious experiment for her to string together a coherent sentence.

She blinked and fought valiantly to focus her mind on the task ahead. Lord knows, no New York newspaper would ever touch her if she couldn't even conjure up the words to put together one measly little fluff article.

She closed her eyes, gifting herself with one more minute to remember the way Sam touched her, promising herself after sixty blissful seconds, she'd focus her thoughts and pull her article together before tomorrow's deadline.

As her lids slipped shut, heated memories of how Sam's hands caressed her naked flesh, pushing, pulling, raising her passion higher and higher, drawing her in deeper until she was drowning in pleasure, rushed through her mind.

Skin flushed from heat and desire, Cat pressed her fingers into her thighs and squeezed as she thought about all those strategically placed mirrors. Her body quaked just thinking how Sam went to so much trouble to seduce her mind as well as her body. Her skin moistened. Her pulse leapt. A small moan crawled out of her throat.

She remembered the way her breasts trembled as Sam lapped at her, making slow, skilled passes over her nipples with the soft blade of his tongue. She clamped her legs together as they began to quiver with yearning.

Cat recalled Sam's deep hypnotic voice and the way he coaxed her to let go and enjoy. Not that there had been much coaxing going on.

Cat inhaled, but what she drew into her lungs was not delectable memories of Sam's heady aroma. The offensive scent of cheap aftershave assaulted her senses and pulled her from her musings. Passion receding, she blinked her eyes open. Out of her peripheral saw Eric Hawkins crane his neck around the fabricated divider separating their desks.

Oh joy.

Of course, she knew it had to be Hawk; no one else in the office reeked of cheesy cologne. He reminded her of that cartoon skunk Pepe Le Peu, with ribbons of his funky scent billowing behind like a cloud of dust.

"Eric," she greeted through clenched teeth, refusing to give in and call him Hawk, no matter how much he insisted.

He leaned forward, his dark hair cloaking his beady eyes. "Rough morning?" he asked, gaze panning the length of her. "You were making strange noises."

Cat shivered and folded her arms, her skin crawling from his physical inspection.

"No," she said flatly, shifting in her seat, making it clear with her body language that she had no interest in pursuing a conversation with him.

He wasn't deterred. Hawk grabbed his jeans, right around the vicinity of his crotch, and tugged before propping himself onto the corner of her desk. Cat resisted the urge to retch.

This *man*, and she used that term loosely, barely two years older than her, assumed his senior position gave him pull with the ladies, inside the office and out. He strutted the streets like he was God's gift to women. Lord, if Hawk was the gift, Cat hated to see the consolation prize.

Hawk raked his hand through his black hair, pushing it off his forehead. "It appears that little article of yours sure has caused a lot of trouble for that scientist." The man wasn't known for his subtleness.

Cat grumbled something incoherent under her breath.

He inched closer, until his thigh touched her arm. "I could probably talk Blain into letting you write another one." When she met his glance, Hawk shot her a suggestive look.

She watched as he toyed with his pen, an annoying little habit he had. Cat gripped her coffee cup tighter, resisting the urge to grab that pen from him and pierce a hole in his over-inflated ego.

The truth was, Cat had asked Blain to let her write another piece, to clear up the media's erroneous take on her first article. Unfortunately, Blain refused to let her follow up on the story, insisting she keep to her "Cat on the Prowl" articles because that's what the readers expected from her. The only reason he had let her try her hand at an article in the first place was to appease her after months of hassling him.

Of course, it occurred to her if she wrote a follow-up and managed to convince activists Sam wasn't testing the serum on Rio, he'd no longer need her assistance for his experiment. As much as she knew another night with him would be her emotional undoing, she couldn't help herself. She needed to be with him again as much as she needed her next breath.

"So what do you say, Kitty-Cat?"

Her head snapped up. "I told you not to call me that."

Ignoring her, he continued. "Do you want me to talk to Blain for you?"

As much as she'd like to write another article, she didn't want any favors from Hawk. God only knew what he would want in return. She shivered just thinking about it.

He lowered his voice and leaned in. His eyes skirted over her once again. "Come on, Cat. You really need to start being a *player* if you want to get ahead in this competitive business. Come out with me Saturday night and we'll talk about the ways I can help you."

She'd rather pull her toenails off with a pair of pliers than spend a Saturday night with him.

Feeling compelled to show him exactly what she thought

of his nauseating idea, she slammed her coffee cup onto her desk with much more force than required. The coffee sloshed over the sides and landed on Hawk's jeans. Such a shame.

With bright-eyed innocence, she blinked up at him. "Oh, sorry."

Hawk jumped and swatted at his crotch. Likely the most action that area had seen in awhile. That small stunt might have earned her a scowl from him, but it gave her a whole lot of self-satisfaction.

His jaw clenched and his nostrils flared as his beady eyes tracked back to her face. "You know, Cat," he bit out, "a second article might have given you a chance to impress the editors at the *Daily Press*. You're screwing your own career."

Better than screwing him.

Wait! Her mind raced. How did he know about the *Daily Press*? Before she had a chance to ask, he turned his back to her and strutted away. Refusing to give him satisfaction by chasing after him, she sat in her chair and stewed.

Well, that hadn't gone quite as planned. Grumbling, Cat turned her attention back to her blank screen. Returning to professional mode, she dug into her interview notes and re-directed her attention to this week's column.

A short while later, Cat blinked her eyes and was pleased to see she'd written a good chunk of her article. She scanned it, thrilled to discover it wasn't half bad. Actually, it was pretty damn good.

As she read it over again, she found herself chuckling out loud, realizing just how much she enjoyed writing about mating and dating woes. She had to admit, when she hit the big times, she would miss frequenting the nightclubs and mingling with the young and well-hung, as she'd once heard it put. Cat enjoyed interviewing both genders on their dating disasters. Not that she had to frequent the clubs for research material, she just enjoyed the interaction. Lately, however, her phone had been ringing off the hook with people wanting to tell their stories to her. She had enough research material and ideas to last a whole year.

Cat climbed from her chair and stretched. Her gaze skated over the office, taking stock of her coworkers milling about, phones ringing, and televisions blaring as everyone kept a close eye on current events. It was only a small setup compared to the *Daily Press*, but most of the people in the office were her friends. She kind of liked the close-knit family feel to it. Perhaps it was because she'd grown accustomed to having so many people around, being raised in a family with six older brothers and all.

Her gaze fell on the floor-to-ceiling glass wall separating the office complex from the bustling downtown sidewalk. The midday autumn sun sliced through the clear panels and beckoned her. Since she needed to grab lunch and stretch her legs, she decided to answer the call of the warm rays. As she made her way to the door, she spotted her boss, Blain, seated in his office.

She stopped and backtracked. "Do you have a minute?"

Blain glanced up from his keyboard, his kind brown eyes meeting her gaze. In some ways he reminded her of her father. Perhaps it was the short cut hair and tinges of gray around his temples. Blain played hardball with his staff, needing to run a tight ship, but Cat knew deep down he was a fair man.

"That depends," he replied.

They both knew the real reason she stood there, clinging to his doorframe like a barnacle, so there really was no point in skirting the issue. "So what do you say? Have you changed your mind about me doing a follow-up?"

"No."

Cat stepped farther into the office. "Come on, Blain. My article was great and you know it." Except for the fact that she made one teeny, tiny mistake and mentioned Rio, of course.

"That's not the point, Cat."

"Then what is the point?" she asked, willing to play hardball in return to get what she wanted.

Blain drew air and leaned back in his chair. "Are we going to do this again?"

Cat planted her hands on her hips; her lips thinned. "Sam is a good guy. He doesn't deserve to have protestors breathing down his neck. Let me write another article to make this right for him."

Cat stiffened as Hawk's voice sounded from behind. "Sounds like someone is sweet on Mr. Scientist."

She spun around and met with dark eyes that burned into her like hot coals. One brow arched knowingly. He gave a derisive twist of his lips, his voice taking on a hard edge. "Is this article really about Sam, or is it about you, Cat?"

"Hawk," Blain's voice grated in warning, obviously tasting the tension between the two.

Contrary to what Hawk believed, the article was intended to benefit Sam, not herself. This was no longer about personal gain or upping her credentials to impress the *Daily Press*, which made her take pause. Wouldn't a hard-core journalist use whatever means necessary to fetch a story? Even go against their own best interests, or step on a few people along the way? Some inner voice warned that, contrary to what her father believed or wanted, perhaps she wasn't cut out for hard-hitting news after all.

Ignoring Hawk, Cat turned back to Blain and switched tactics. "One article, then I'll drop it."

"It's too late, Cat. Yesterday I asked Hawk to do a follow-up. He's on it."

Cat's lips tightened. Anger flared through her. She twisted around and cut Hawk a look, resisting the urge to whack that smirk off his face. The lying bastard had no intention of talking to Blain for her, like he'd offered earlier, in return for God knows what. He'd known all along he'd gotten the follow-up.

She walked up to Hawk and pinned him with a glare. "You make this right for Sam." With that she stalked back to her desk. Mind racing, she stared at her half-finished article for the next fifteen minutes or so, yet couldn't seem to concentrate on a single word. Agitated, she rifled through her drawers, although she had no idea what she was searching for.

Her stomach grumbled, reminding her of her destination before she'd gotten sidetracked. Needing air, she grabbed an orange off her desk, pulled her tote bag out from beside her chair, and made her way to the front door.

As she approached the glass wall, she glanced out and spotted Hawk talking to someone on the other side of the street. The man looked vaguely familiar. Cat squinted, her mind racing, trying to place the guy Hawk appeared to be in deep conversation with. Then it hit her. It was none other than the infamous protester, Eugene Letterman.

She furrowed her brow in confusion. Why would Hawk be talking to Eugene?

Cat's stomach tightened. She felt her blood run cold. She didn't like the look of this at all. Not one little bit. Hawk was up to something. Every instinct warned her. Did this have something to do with Sam? Were the two in cahoots? If so, how and for how long?

Cat ripped the peel off her orange and moved closer to the window, wishing she could hear their distant conversation. Hawk handed something to Eugene, but from her angle and distance she couldn't tell what.

Perhaps it was time for her to do a little investigation of her own, whether Blain approved or not.

Chapter 6

With all the metered spots taken in front of Cat's newspaper office, Sam parked a block down the street and walked the rest of the way. The warm sun beat down on him and helped soothe his ragged nerves. As he approached her building, he spotted Cat pushing through the front glass door and stepping out onto the curb. The minute Sam set eyes on her his body buzzed to life and his blood raced.

South.

He registered every curvy detail of her business attire. Coat draped over her arm, she wore a knee-length black skirt that hugged her hips in all the right places and a soft green blouse that matched the color of her eyes. Cat scanned the street and ripped the peel off an orange like the two had a personal vendetta.

What was it with her and oranges anyway, he mused. Did she have some kind of addiction?

Sam could almost smell the succulent wedges. He could almost taste its vine-ripened sweetness.

He could *almost* stop his cock from hardening.

Damn.

Twirling on the ball of her foot, Cat spun in the opposite direction and hurried down the street. He had no idea where she was headed, but her strides appeared to be quite determined.

"Cat," Sam called out to her, but the bustling pedestrians and street sounds swallowed his voice. Weaving his way through the lunch-hour crowd, he jogged to catch up. As his long legs ate up the distance, he called out again, louder this time.

Her footsteps stilled. She turned back around. Her mouth dropped open but no words came. He could almost hear a small gasp crawl out of her throat when she spotted him rushing toward her.

Smoothing her hair off her face, a gesture he was becoming increasingly accustomed to, Cat hitched her bag higher on her shoulder and stepped toward him.

"Sam. What are you doing here?" He'd been the one jogging, yet she was the one who sounded winded.

Gorgeous cat eyes widened with a mixture of delight and surprise as she studied him. His heart skipped a beat, thrilled with the way she reacted upon seeing him, and equally thrilled that there was no awkwardness between them after last night.

He touched her arm. He wasn't exactly sure why. He'd never been the needy, touchy feely type with women before. But Cat was so damn irresistible he couldn't keep his hands off her. Then again, there was always the possibility he was seeking some deeper form of intimacy with her.

Sam frowned in concentration.

"Is something wrong?" she asked, her perfect brow arching with genuine concern. She placed her hand on his forearm and squeezed, a silent offering of support and comfort.

Tenderness stole over him. The warmth in her eyes spoke volumes. Cat Nichols, the same woman who'd written an article on him and unknowingly fucked his future, really and truly cared about his well-being. It touched him somewhere down deep, stirring up old feelings. As bewitching green cat eyes stared up at him in worry, he felt a flash of possessiveness.

Guilt washed over him like a tsunami wave, guilt for even entertaining the idea that she'd offered herself in exchange just to get the story.

"Sam?" she asked again, "Are you okay?"

It took a moment for him to remember why he was there. He searched his mind and remembered the note. Yes, the note, the reason he'd braved lunch-hour traffic and darted down the street after her like a crazed junkie looking for a fix. Not his desperate need to see her, to touch her, to kiss her, or to hold her in his arms again.

He drew a breath, centering himself, and addressed her worries. "I need to talk to you about a letter I received today," he answered, knowing damn well he was skirting the truth.

She angled her body and peered around his shoulder. She closed her eyes for a brief second and drew in air. "Oh no," she whispered.

Reading her distress, Sam twisted around, his gaze brushed over the crowd. "What is it?"

Cat dropped her orange into her tote bag and grabbed his arm, alarm in her expression. "Remember that loud-mouthed protestor?" Without giving him time to answer, she jerked her head to Sam's left and rushed on, "Well he's coming our way."

A surge of anger made Sam's blood boil. With both hands fisted, he made a move to turn, but Cat stopped him as though reading his intent.

Why the hell was he such an easy read lately anyway?

"Not here, Sam," she warned. "Not in front of the paper. Not unless you want to be tomorrow's headline."

Blood pounding, he ground his back teeth together until his jaw ached. "I don't."

"I didn't think so. Come with me." Cat tugged on his arm and led him into an alleyway.

With little choice in the matter, Sam complied and high-tailed it down the street behind her. Like a dog on the chase, he followed Cat between two towering buildings.

"Where are we going?" His voice came out gruff, hating that he had to dart from the protestor, especially if the son of a bitch was responsible for the threatening note. Even though he would have preferred to get to the bottom of this, here and now, gut instinct told him avoiding a direct confrontation was his best course of action. The last thing he needed was his name splashed across the morning headlines, especially when the media attention had just begun to die down.

"There's a back door to the office. We'll go in there and wait it out." Cat reached into her tote bag and pulled out her identification card. She ran it through an electronic lock and pushed the heavy metal door open. "In here."

She stepped in and Sam followed. With her fingers pressed to her lips she whispered, "I'm not supposed to be doing this, so don't make any noise."

He put his mouth close to her ear. The scent of succulent orange and fruity shampoo reached his nostrils. He inhaled. Damn, he could just eat her up and go back for seconds. "I don't want to get you into trouble," he whispered.

She mouthed the words, "It's okay. Follow me."

Shadowing her, Sam stepped into what appeared to be a small storage room.

"The door, Sam—"

Before she had a chance to finish her sentence, Sam gripped the knob, and with a hard tug, pulled the wooden door shut behind them, blanketing them in darkness.

"Sam, no."

Confused by the distress in her tone, he turned in the direction of her voice. "What?"

Cat groaned. "Tell me you didn't pull that tight."

Obviously missing something, Sam blinked, trying to focus on her, but unable to see anything in the pitch dark. "I'm afraid I can't do that."

Cat cursed under her breath. Sexy little breathy cussing words that actually turned him on. Not that it took much these days. Christ, what kind of a guy got turned on by swearing? Actually, it really didn't matter what Cat said. She could scream at him in a foreign language and it would still arouse him. Just the sound of her melodic voice turned him on.

Wouldn't Doctor Phil have a field day with that one?

"The latch is broken," she said.

Sam felt her slide past him, enjoying the way her body brushed against his. She toyed with the door handle then blew out a resigned breath.

"Great. We're stuck."

"Stuck?"

"Yeah, stuck. The latch is broken and the damn door-frame is swollen from all the rain and high humidity we've had recently. Maintenance was supposed to be here two days ago. They're not known for their promptness."

Sam tried the door. It didn't budge. He put his shoulder into it but to no avail; it still didn't open. Running his hand along the wall, Sam groped for a light switch. "Now I suppose you're going to tell me the light is burnt out too."

Cat flicked the switch. Sam blinked and winced. "Thanks for the warning."

She shot him an apologetic glance. "Sorry." Turning her attention to her tote bag, she rooted through it and pulled out her half-peeled orange, setting it on top of the filing cabinet.

The arousing scent assailed his senses and curled around him, bringing back heated memories of the intoxicating taste of her mouth, and the unique feminine taste between her thighs.

Sam's stomach growled. His mouth salivated as his hunger for her clawed its way to the surface. His dick grew hard. A slow burning fire trickled through his veins.

He watched Cat, hair falling forward, intense concentration on her face. His heart did a curious little jump as her beauty stole his next breath. Her pretty pink tongue darted out and swiped at her bottom lip. God, she looked so gorgeous. Her sensual movements bombarded him with foreign emotions. His muscles tightened with lust and need.

"What are you doing?" His voice came out a little deep, a little gruff as he envisioned himself getting reacquainted with those luscious lips of hers.

Both sets.

Sam had the distinct impression that if he touched her again, kissed her, and sank his engorged cock into her slick heat, it would ultimately get the little wildcat deeper into his system, not out, like he'd originally anticipated. He should pull back, he really should. Before they crossed some imaginary intimacy line and she touched him on another level.

She sounded flustered. "I'm looking for my cell phone. I have to call someone to get us out." She shivered. "I'm claustrophobic."

Sam reached into his jeans, his fingers curling around his cell phone. He pressed a button, turning it off.

"Where the hell is my phone?" Cat grumbled under her breath as pens and notepads spilled to the floor.

It occurred to Sam that calling for help was not his first priority. He swallowed and stepped closer, crowding her. So much for his plan to pull back. Around Cat he became blindsided by need and his control crumbled like burnt toast.

Anticipation coursed through him as his gaze flitted across her body. He felt a rush of sexual energy, similar to the one he'd gotten in Jessica Johnson's little kissing closet back in junior high. It felt as naughtily delicious now as it did back then. Only this time, kissing wouldn't even begin to sate his hunger.

Taking pause, Sam considered their predicament a moment longer. Two hours ago he'd never expected to be locked in a storage closet with Cat, sporting the mother of all boners. He had to admit, his day was taking a turn for the better.

"Are you telling me no one can get in or out? That we could be stuck in here for hours?" His mind raced and filled with all the deliciously wicked things he could do to that lush body in those few hours.

She snorted and gave him a look suggesting he was two pages behind. "Haven't you been listening?"

He grinned, enjoying this sassy side of her. "I've been listening," he assured her. "I just wanted to be sure of the details."

Still searching her bag, she wrinkled her nose, impatience obvious in her stance. "Details? What are you talking about, Sam?"

He moved into her personal space and adjusted his footing, until her legs were trapped inside his. "Maybe you shouldn't call just yet." His words sounded suggestive and gained her attention.

She flicked him a glance. When her gaze met his, her movements stilled, awareness dawning on her face. "Oh."

Her eyes lit up, obviously reading the passion brewing inside him and rising to the surface.

Gaze riveted, he smiled a slow sensual smile that told her in no uncertain terms the naughtily delicious idea he was entertaining.

Her breathing grew shallow, her green eyes clouded. Straightening her spine, she made a move to push her hair off her face. Sam reached out and stopped her, liking the way it hung forward, the tips brushing over her nipples. Nipples that had, under his smoldering gaze, started to swell and poke against her thin silk blouse.

As he concentrated on those luscious peaks, his grin dissolved. The air around them charged. Sam had never felt such a powerful pull before. The chemistry between them was explosive, unlike anything he'd ever experienced.

His voice dropped an octave. "I was thinking, Cat." He surfed his finger over her cheek, and lower, over her blouse, stopping around the vicinity of her first button. "If we're going to be locked in here for hours, I was thinking we should use this window of opportunity to test your responses again." He got quiet for a moment, letting her digest the information and warm to the idea. Then, as an afterthought, he added, "Since we blew it last night."

"Twice," Cat added with a nervous, yet anticipatory giggle.

Sexual energy jetted between them and heated the room. Sam twined his arm around her, tugged her blouse out from her skirt, and splayed his fingers over the small of her back. His thumb stole over her sensitive skin in a gentle brush. She shuddered as her flesh came alive from his intimate caress. He loved the way she wanted him, the way her body beckoned his touch.

"Mmm, you're so soft, Cat." The heat from her naked flesh reached out to him and seeped under his skin as he pulled her impossibly closer, anchoring her curvy hips to his.

Cat's hands joined the play. She put them on either side of his waist and pressed against him. Her lashes fluttered as she tipped her chin to look into his eyes.

"Sam, we're in the storage closet at my work." Her voice had taken on a sultry, sexy edge. "This is risky." Her protest lacked conviction, and they both knew it. "What if we get caught?" Sam noted that her words said one thing, but the curiosity and excitement dancing in her eyes told an entirely different story.

"What if we don't?" His rough voice gave way to soft persuasion. Fueled by need, he put his mouth close to hers. Their breaths mingled.

Cat got quiet for a moment and then her gaze traveled to his eyes, assessing him. "So this is for work, Sam? For research?" Her breathy whisper covered him like a warm summer breeze, giving him goose bumps. She'd actually given him goose bumps, for Christ sake. No one had ever given him goose bumps before.

Sam suddenly felt as if his whole world shifted when her honest, honey-flecked eyes searched his for answers. The connection between them was tremendous and he knew his need for her was reaching an all new high.

"No," he answered, deciding she deserved the truth. "I want you, Cat," he admitted honestly. "I've wanted you for a long time now."

Her eyes dimmed with desire. She smiled up at him. Something about the intimate, emotional way she looked at him nearly stopped his heart.

"I want you too, Sam."

He dipped his head and filled his lungs with her scent. "Good," he whispered into her hair, pulling and pushing at her clothes, hands skimming her curves, unable to get enough. Her soft purr resonated through his body. "Then I'm all yours. You may do with me as you wish," he said, his voice full of teasing warmth. "And don't feel the need to be gentle." Sam grabbed her bag and slipped it from her shoulder, letting it fall to the floor with a clunk, forgotten. "Because sometimes I like it rough."

"Only one problem," Cat said.

He slid his fingers through her hair and angled her head. He pressed his mouth into the hollow of her throat and breathed a kiss over her skin. Cat moaned and arched into him.

His heart pounded erratically. God, he needed to touch

her and taste her all over. He gave a low growl then rushed on. "No Cat, trust me, there's no problem. Everything is perfect," he assured her, certain that if she stopped him, the heat coursing through his veins would cause him to go up in a burst of flames. "Turn that inquisitive mind of yours off and stop thinking."

"But you said I had to wait twenty-four hours between stimulation before I can take the serum. If you *stimulate* me now, I won't be able to take the serum tonight."

God, it was just like her to be concerned about his future at a time like this. It warmed him to the depths of his soul. Cat Nichols probably wasn't the kind of girl who'd up and leave a guy when something *bigger and better* came along either. Whoa! Where had that thought come from? Waging a war with his emotions, Sam pushed that thought far away, not wanting to go there, just wanting to enjoy each other for the moment before it all disappeared. And it would disappear. It always did. He'd learned long ago, he didn't have what it took to keep a woman around.

With a long savoring stroke, he licked her neck and inhaled her intoxicating scent. He ached to taste every inch of her skin and lose himself in her again and again.

His whole body trembled, his voice coming out shaky. "I guess that just means we'll have to go for round three tomorrow night. Because baby, I plan on stimulating you. At least a couple of times." A thin sheen of perspiration pebbled his flesh as his mind conjured up the numerous ways to accomplish such a delightful task.

He could feel her pulse beat in a mad cadence beneath his tongue. A fever rose in him, forcing him to take a fortifying breath and summon a modicum of control. Fuck . . . he needed to slow down before he lost it and came right there, with his jeans still on.

She tried to voice an argument. "But Sam . . ." Her voice trailed off when he reached between her legs and in one quick motion snapped the thin elastic on her panties.

No matter what she thought, there was no way she was getting out of that room before he buried his face between her legs and tasted her sweetness. He knew it, and it was time she knew it too.

He parted her soft folds.

"You were saying?" Sam asked.

"What . . ." she stammered, her words fractured. It took effort for her to speak. Sam smiled, taking great satisfaction in his ability to shut down that inquisitive mind of hers. "What . . . what about your deadline?" she sounded so winded, her voice full of want.

"My what?" God, he couldn't think now either. Not with her full breasts poking into his chest. And the way she swayed her hips, ever so slightly, grinding her lush pussy on his finger, snapped his last vestige of control.

Cat pushed her hands through his hair and linked her

fingers behind his head, holding on for support. A violent shudder overtook him as her touch seeped under his skin.

"Your–" Her words died away when she felt the way his body reacted to her touch. Her sounds of protest morphed into a heated moan.

A shiver prowled through him. "I want you, Cat." He hungered for her with an intensity that made his hands shake.

She gave a broken gasp. *"Sam . . ."* There was such urgency and emotion in her voice.

"Cat, babe, you need to stop talking so I can kiss you." Driven by need his lips crashed down on hers. She opened for him as he feasted on her lips. He loved the way she kissed him. Her lips were warm and silky and made him ache to kiss the other dewy set at the apex of her legs, ache to drink in her intoxicating tang of arousal.

Sam's muscles bunched. His balls tightened. His tongue slipped inside her mouth for a frenzied exploration. The warmth of her mouth made his knees buckle.

His finger dipped into her heated core, then stroked back and forth over her swollen clit, repeating the motion until her body shook. He plucked at her delicate pearl, making it swell with need, begging to be kissed and stroked, nibbled and nipped.

Her aroused scent called out to him. His nostrils flared, eager to answer that call, aching to drop to his knees and taste her liquid silk.

Cat broke the kiss, inched back, and drew a breath. Sam's hand slipped from between her legs. Mischief danced in her eyes as they locked on his. Her mouth curved wickedly, her face flushed from heat and desire. "Oh and just for the record, Sam. I didn't blow anything last night. Definitely an oversight on my part." Her hand went to his throbbing dick and squeezed. There was a suggestive edge to her smile. "One I believe I'd like to rectify."

Sweet mother of God!

So she wanted to play sex games with him, did she?

Her bold words prompted him into action. Trembling from head to toe, Sam grabbed her arms and walked her backwards, trapping her between his body and the wall. He pushed his cock against her, holding her in place. Her body molded against his as his gaze traveled to her breasts. Dark nipples tightened with arousal and poked out at him. A low growl of longing that didn't even sound human gathered in his throat as his hands cupped her orbs. Thank God, the thick door buffered their sex sounds.

Using slow circular motions that drove Cat wild, he brushed her pebbled nubs through her blouse.

Christ, he needed to slow things down before he erupted on the spot. He inched back, giving them both a bit of breathing room.

He heard the raw ache of lust in her voice. "Sam, you

wouldn't happen to have a couple of condoms in your wallet would you?"

"I'm afraid not." In fact, it had been a long time since he needed one.

Cat tilted her head and looked around, almost frantic, her eyes full of urgent need. "This is a storage room. Maybe we can find something in here."

Sam chuckled and followed her gaze. His glance came to rest on her forgotten orange. He bit back a wicked grin, conjuring up a few sex games of his own.

"Yes, maybe we can find something to use," he agreed as the most delicious plan began to formulate in his mind.

Face flushed, Cat licked her lips and swallowed. Hard. At that moment Sam realized just how hot it had gotten in the small room.

He frowned in concern. "Are you okay?" he whispered, brushing her hair from her face.

She drew a shaky breath. "Parched. My bag. Water bottle."

Sam chuckled, loving the way he got to her. He pried her legs open with his knee. "Don't move," he warned in a soft, yet commanding voice.

"You really are very bossy, you know."

He grinned. "I know." Leaving her pressed against the wall, legs spread wide, he snatched her bag from the floor and opened it.

"You know, Sam. A man is never supposed to go into a woman's bag."

He peered inside. "Really?"

"Yeah, really."

"Why?" he asked as her rooted through the contents. He dug through a ton of papers, pens, cosmetics, and other things he'd rather not know what she used for, in his quest to find her water bottle. "Is it because we're unable to find things with all this junk?"

"It's not junk," she said, feigning hurt.

He pulled out a smooth round rock. His lips twitched as he and held it up to her. "No?"

She furrowed her brow in mock annoyance. "Hey, that's not junk. My nephew Matt gave me that." She laughed, low and throaty. Then her voice dropped an octave, her lids lowered. "It's because it's personal, Sam. Going through a woman's bag is personal."

He lowered his voice to match hers and cast a long lingering glance. "And this isn't?" he asked, slowly sliding his thumb up her leg and under her skirt until he found her swollen clit. He brushed his thumb over it, slowly, methodically, making her writhe and moan in heavenly bliss. He dipped one finger inside. Her pussy clamped around him as he stirred her heat.

She braced herself against the wall. Her breathing hitched;

her lids slipping shut. "Oh, my," she said in an unsteady voice.

"Now do you want me to find your water bottle or not," he gruffed, humor edging his voice.

Sam noted the dots of perspiration on her forehead. With unabashed passion, she pushed her pelvis against him and said, "Not if it means you're going to stop doing that."

In one fluid motion, Sam grabbed her hand and placed it on her clit. Taking her index finger in his, he swiped it over her passion-drenched sex. Her lids flew open. Her jaw dropped and she stared at him in mute surprise. Sam smiled at her. "Why don't you take over for me for a second." It was a command, not a question.

She let out an excited rush of breath and read the real reason behind his actions. "Do you like this, Sam? Do you like watching?" she asked, her voice full of tortured promise as the gleam in her eye turned wicked.

Lust exploded through him. The sweet torment made him throb. His cock pressed so hard against his jeans it hurt to the point of pain. But it was a pain he was willing to put up with to watch Cat pleasure herself. Damned if he didn't like that.

"Does this turn you on, Sam?" Her voice was low, husky.

He gulped. A shiver skittered through him. "Hell, yeah."

A low groan sounded in her throat as she swooshed her fingers over her clit. She hiked her skirt up and spread her pink lips wider, giving him his own personal peep show. The sight of her damp, passion-soaked curls and the scent of her arousal saturated the room. Sam inhaled, drawing it into his lungs, letting it curl through his body and bring warmth to the darkest corners.

As her scent rushed through his bloodstream, his body responded with urgent demands and he almost lost it right then and there. His throat dried. Blood pounded through his veins as he fully appreciated her private seduction. Vibrating with need, Sam finally found the water bottle, wishing he could pour the cold liquid over his body, one part in particular.

Almost desperate, he pulled on the plastic spout and squeezed it into his mouth. "Damn, it's not working."

"You don't squeeze, Sam. You suck. Let me show you." With her free hand, she took the bottle from him, wrapped her lips around the plastic spout and sucked, long and hard.

Oh. My. Fuck.

Sam stood there, barely able to move, barely able to breathe, watching as she pleasured herself and sucked on the bottle, the exact same way he wanted her to suck on his cock.

A moment later, after she had her fill, she handed it back to him and licked a drop from her lips. He grabbed the bottle and took a long pull. Letting the cool water ease the heat inside him.

"Do you want more?" *Lord, was that his voice? He sounded like he'd just eaten a bucket of nails.*

"One more sip," she said. Sam held the bottle to her lips while she drank. There was something very intimate in sharing a water bottle, he decided.

After she finished, he twisted around and placed the bottle on the filing cabinet.

"Thank you, Sam," she said in a soft tone.

He turned back to her. When he met her eyes, desire for something more, something deeper twisted inside him. Sam sucked in a shaky breath and watched her for a moment. As his gaze panned her body, everything in him reached out to her.

"Sam."

Her voice gained his attention. His eyes went to hers. "Yeah?"

She pulled her hand out from under her skirt. Her eyes panned his body like a sultry caress. "I'm very, very wet." Her finger went to her mouth.

He scrubbed a rough hand over his jaw. "Jesus Christ, Cat. Are you trying to turn me into a premature ejaculator?"

Her soft chuckle curled around him. She crooked her finger and motioned him closer.

Her finger went back to her mouth as Sam wrapped his arms around her, pinning her to his body. He closed his mouth over hers, taking her finger and her tongue into his mouth at the same time.

With his throbbing cock pressed against her, he gyrated, aching for something far more intimate. Cat tore at his shirt and ripped it from his pants. Without haste, Sam pulled it off and tossed it aside.

He listened as she inhaled, taking his scent into her lungs. Soft silken lips found his chest. She kissed his naked skin and made small sexy bedroom noises as she indulged in the taste of him. Her hot tongue lapped at his nipples with determined strokes, branding him with her heat.

He wrapped his hands around her, cushioning her in his arms as a strange primal possessive sound climbed out of his throat. Cat's soft lips met with his again, kissing him with all the passion inside her, feeding the intensity of his arousal. Small hands reached for the button on his jeans.

Locking his knees, Sam groaned and gripped her shoulders.

Eyes dark with desire, she popped the button and lowered his zipper. One small hand slipped inside and glided over his swollen head. It pulsed and jerked in response. The first sweet stroke of her delicate fingers on his cock shut down his ability to think.

Her tongue darted out to moisten her lips. She glanced up at him, eyes gleaming wickedly, her tone playful. "Mmmm, very nice, Sam. Very responsive," she murmured, turning her attention back to his chest, kissing him with wild abandonment.

With his cock encased in her warm exploring hands, he grew impossibly harder.

Did she have any idea what her teasing did to him?

Heat radiated from her fingers as she squeezed and stroked and dipped into the fluid dripping from the slit.

He couldn't explain it. In fact, he didn't understand it. Other women had touched him in the same manner, but there was something special in the way she touched him. It was the most intimate thing he'd ever felt.

As Cat leaned into him, long blonde curls fell over his body in silken waves, tickling his flesh, bringing his arousal to new heights. Barely able to breathe, let alone move, Sam stood there, absorbing her heat, enjoying the way her hands played with his cock. He somehow managed to smooth her hair back to watch her, enjoying the seductive way she touched him, until the pressure building in his body became too much for him to bear.

He grabbed her wrists and stopped her. "Cat, stop." His voice came out harsher than he intended.

Gorgeous eyes blinked up at him. "You don't like it?"

God, when he looked into her eyes, he felt like he was drowning. He gulped for his next breath. "Oh, I like it, babe. I like it a lot. Too much, in fact. You see, you've got me so turned on, one more stroke and I'm going to lose it. And I'm not ready to lose it just yet, sweetheart. I want to taste you first. It's all I can think about." His voice was raw with lust and need.

Her chest heaved. "Oh, okay," she agreed, nodding her head, not even bothering to mask her enthusiasm.

Sam chuckled. God, he loved her like this. Loving how open and relaxed they were with each other. Loving how easy she was to be with.

His thumb went to her nipple, stroking her through the fabric. "Doesn't seem fair that I'm half naked and you're not." He popped one button. Her face flushed darker, anticipation sparkling in her eyes.

"Not fair at all, Sam," she agreed, her head lolling to the side. "And you know I like to play fair," she added, drawing a ragged breath.

He popped another and another until her blouse fell open, exposing a sexy, white lace bra and a long column of silken skin. His gaze settled on her supple cleavage.

"Mmmm. Very nice." Leaning in, he put his mouth between her breasts and brushed his tongue over her tender flesh. "Tell me, Cat. Where were you going in such a hurry?"

She frowned and looked at him, her expression perplexed. "What?" she asked, practically panting as he worked his tongue over her gorgeous breasts. "What are you talking about, Sam?"

"When I met up with you on the sidewalk, where were you going?" His thumb slipped inside her bra and stroked one nipple.

She moaned. "To get lunch," she whispered.

"And I interrupted you?" Sam slipped his index in and caught her nipple between his fingers, pinching and rolling until it swelled.

"It was a good interruption," she rushed out.

He gripped the material of her bra and pulled it down, tucking it under her breasts. He took a moment to just stare at the beautiful erotic sight before him.

He cupped her full breasts and gave a gentle squeeze. "It was an interruption all the same. You must still be hungry, and to think we're going to be locked in here for hours."

Her words faltered as her hands moved to her chest, joining him. The pad of her thumbs played over her tight nipples. "Yes . . . no . . . I don't know. What was the question again?"

Gaze locked on the action, Sam watched her fingers brush over her tight peaks. God, he could barely think.

He dipped his head and made a slow pass with his tongue. "I think you should eat something, to keep up your strength."

He pitched his voice low and put his mouth close to her ear. "I believe you're going to need all your strength, Cat."

That seemed to pique her interest. He felt her tremble and her hands moved faster over her breasts, as though attempting to relieve the deep ache at the core of her body.

Her voice thinned to a whisper. "I . . . I don't have any food, Sam."

Sam stepped back and grabbed the orange from the filing cabinet. The second the scent reached him, his cock pulsed. Who knew an orange could be such a powerful aphrodisiac? He liked oranges but had never gone out of his way to get one before. Now he associated the taste and scent with Cat; he craved them with fierce intensity.

"You know, Cat. You've been driving me crazy, tasting and smelling like a succulent, vine-ripened orange, so sweet, so tempting. It's all I can think about. I can barely work, I can barely sleep. I've spent hours thinking about popping a wedge into my mouth, biting, nibbling, letting the juice slide over my tongue as it quenches my thirst." He rolled the orange between his hands and touched the cool peel to her skin. His knuckles purposely brushed against her pebbled nipples. Her body shuddered, almost uncontrollably.

Cat's dark lashes fluttered. Her face took on a ruddy hue as she made a sexy noise and shifted, hanging on his every word.

Sam ripped into the peeling. "I think it's only fair that I drive you just as crazy. Don't you?" The fresh, fruity, sensual aroma filled the room and fired his craving. He pulled off a wedge, juice trickling down his hand. He licked it off, slowly, lapping at it with long luxurious stokes, long strokes that turned into small quick laps, making no secret about what he wanted to do to her most intimate areas.

Her lips parted. Her breath came in a ragged burst. "Ohmigod, Sam."

Sam brought the wedge to her mouth. Cat put her hands on his shoulders, her fingers biting into his flesh. Sam rubbed the slice over her lips, letting the juice trickle down her chin. Cat's tongue darted out, licking the droplets.

"Mmmm, delicious," she murmured.

Sam popped the wedge into her mouth and nudged her chin up with his thumb. Leaning in, he rained kisses over her lips and neck, lingering there, breathing in her scent and savoring the arousing taste of her. The grip on his shoulders tightened. He inched back and watched her throat as she swallowed.

"Would you undress for me, Cat?" His voice sounded tight.

Without pause, Cat pushed off the wall and slowly slipped her blouse off, letting it fall to the floor.

"Your bra, too."

His body shook and his cock throbbed as she unhooked

her bra, releasing her full breasts from their restrictive confines.

Their gazes locked and held. "Now your skirt." There was an ache of longing in his voice and he wondered if she heard it.

Wiggling her hips, she eased the skirt down. After she kicked it away, she straightened, standing before him completely naked, completely comfortable in her own skin. Small hands reached out to him, her eyes pleading for his touch.

"Sam . . ." she whispered, her voice a sultry invitation.

He called on every ounce of strength not to press her against the wall and fuck her right then. Sam made quick work of his own clothes, needing desperately to feel flesh on flesh, skin on skin.

"Yeah, babe."

"I want you."

"I want you too." Without pause, he closed the distance and took her mouth in his. Their tongues joined and tangled. His hands skimmed her curves as he kissed her long and hard. Moisture sealed their bodies together. Once he had his fill of her mouth, he inched back.

"Are you still hungry?"

Her eyes opened wide, reading his intent. "Starving."

Sam grabbed another wedge of orange. He bit the end off and brought it to her mouth, letting the juice dribble over her lips. Slowly, he dragged the orange over her skin, his tongue following behind, lapping up every single droplet. His body screamed for release as he poised the orange slice over her nipple.

Cat's breath grew shallow.

Eyes fixated on her breasts, Sam squeezed the wedge. Droplets fell and beaded on her tight peaks. As he watched her nipples tighten from the cool juice, his cock throbbed and clamored for attention. He groaned low in his throat.

"So gorgeous," he murmured, stroking the underside of her breasts.

Cat threw her head back and moaned as Sam moved in to lick the droplet. His tongue lapped and swirled around her hard buds until she cried out in heavenly bliss. Cat snaked her hands around his head and arched into him.

Her legs widened. The scent of her arousal beckoned him. Without haste, Sam dropped to his knees and nestled himself between her open legs. Cat ran her fingers through his hair and pitched forward, offering herself to him.

"Sam . . . please," she begged.

He leaned back on his heels and lifted his chin to meet her eyes. "Please what?" he asked, his gaze searching hers.

"Please taste me," came her breathy reply.

"It'd be my pleasure." Sam parted her fold and took a long moment just to look at her luscious pink softness. Desire slammed into him. His heart crashed against his chest as he inhaled her aroused scent in frank appreciation.

He grabbed another wedge of orange and bit the end off. Cat reached down and opened her plump sex lips wider, providing him with easier access.

Her bold behavior nearly undid him. "Jesus," he cursed under his breath, wondering how much more he could take. He'd never been so turned on in his life.

He squeezed juice onto her clit and let it run over her folds. Sam gulped as her sex glistened invitingly.

The cool drops made her body tremble.

"It's cold," she murmured and squirmed against him.

"Then let me warm you up." With a feathery light caress, his tongue sifted through her curls and swirled over her clit. For a long time he rained kisses over her passion-drenched pussy. Her feminine scent, combined with the taste of orange, made his head spin and turned his world inside out. He made another slow pass with his tongue and could feel her muscles tighten and quake.

"I love the way your body responds to me," he whispered.

"And I love what you do to me," she said, and shamelessly bucked her pussy against his face. He drew a ragged breath as her pleasure resonated through him, spurring him on. Hands cupping the lush curve of her ass, he plunged his tongue into her, bringing her closer and closer to climax.

Moaning, Cat rode his tongue, pressing and grinding against him. He held her tighter; her skin felt feverish.

"Sam, God. I want to feel your cock inside me."

Fuck, he wanted that too. Unfortunately, without a condom, he couldn't give them what they both wanted, what they both needed. His hand slid around her hips and moved to her pussy. He pinched her clit and she shuddered, violently.

"More, Sam. Harder." She rocked against him.

His mouth went to her clit. He took it between his teeth and nipped as he slipped two fingers inside her. Cat sucked in a breath as he worked his fingers in and out of her. Changing the pace and rhythm until he could feel small quakes rippling deep inside her.

Beneath his ministrations, her whole body convulsed and Sam knew she was close. His fingers stroked deep as his voice coaxed her on. "Come for me, Cat. Let me taste you." He slipped a third finger into her heated core, filling her as he pressed a hot kiss to her clit.

As he kept up the gentle assault, Sam could feel her orgasm building and pulling at her.

"Oh, Sam. Don't stop. I'm there."

Her erotic whimper filled the room as she gave herself over to her climax. Sam licked her clit harder and increased the tempo of his fingers, nurturing her release, prolonging it, stretching it out for her. He lapped at her and knew he was losing himself in her sweetness.

Sam held her tight as she rode out the last fragments

of her climax. When her muscles stopped quivering, Sam climbed out from between her legs, stood, and dragged her to him, crushing her chest to his. His throat tightened as she melted into him. They held each other for a long while.

He smoothed her hair off her face, put his lips close to her ear, and whispered, "I love the taste of you."

She touched his cheek like it was the most natural thing in the world for her to do. "Doesn't quite seem fair that you got to taste me and I didn't get to taste you." Her hand slipped between their bodies, and sheathed his hard cock. Pleasure raced through him as small fingers squeezed around his engorged erection. He shivered under her touch.

She inched back and glanced into his eyes. They shared a look that touched him somewhere deep inside, bringing another burst of warmth to his darkest corners. Cat brushed her lips lightly over his. Sam's throat tightened when he watched a flurry of emotions pass over her face. His heart raced as his shaky hand reached out and stroked a tender caress over her naked flesh.

"And you know how I like to play fair, Sam."

Rattled, his brain stalled and he worked to speak, to say something coherent, something intelligent. "Yes. It's good to play fair." Hell, intelligence was overrated anyway.

Cat sank to her knees.

Oh fuck.

His cock sprang forward and tangled in Cat's hair as she leaned into him.

His whole body shook as he watched her take a moment to stare at him. Her eyes wide with anticipation, as though taking delight in his rock-hard erection. She touched him, gently. He groaned as his cock pulsed and ached for more. One long finger caressed his swollen head, barely touching as she traced a path down the length of him.

He went absolutely still, knowing that another delicate stroke would push him over the edge. "Cat, babe–" His words fell off when her warm mouth closed over his girth and wrapped around his cock in a wet massage.

"Mmm." She moaned around his phallus, taking him impossibly deeper. Her mouth tightened around him, her teeth scraping lightly as her tongue swirled and lapped with hungry strokes.

She inched back. "I love the taste of you, Sam." Her soft whisper covered him like a blanket of warmth. A barrage of emotions exploded through him.

Cat pressed a kiss to his swollen head, drinking in the juice dripping from his tip. Pressure brewed deep inside him as she answered the pull in his groin.

Hands crushed in her hair, pulling it off her face so he could take pleasure in the sight of her licking his cock. God, her mouth did the most delicious things to him.

"Cat, honey, I'm close," he said, giving her warning, not wanting to come in her mouth.

She continued to work her tongue over him, gifting him with long luxurious licks until he knew he was on the brink of an orgasm. He began rocking his hips, his body seeking release.

Slipping his hand to her chin, he pulled her off and gripped his cock, stroking it once, twice as it pulsed and throbbed with the hot flow of release.

Cat watched as he spurted his seed onto his stomach. She climbed to her feet. Her voice was low, whispery soft, and full of disappointment. "Sam, I wanted to taste you."

His stomach clenched; his heart swelled. "You don't have to do that, Cat." His voice sounded shaky.

Cat grabbed her bag from the floor and pulled out a tissue. "But I wanted to." Her mouth curved as a gleam sparkled in her eyes. "Next time I won't let you stop me," she teased, as she cleaned him up and disposed of the tissue.

Shocked, Sam stood there, his heart racing, watching her clean up after him. The way she chatted so easily about such an intimate matter and the way she acted so cavalier as she wiped away his release, like they'd been lovers their entire lives, did strange things to his insides.

Feeling a little raw and a whole lot vulnerable, he pulled her to him, unable to get her close enough. As her arms snaked around his neck, clinging to him in return, as though she too couldn't get him close enough, Sam realized life as he knew it would never be the same again.

After a long moment, Cat broke the silence. "Sam, do you have any idea what time it is?"

He glanced at his watch and noted that the afternoon had slipped by as they'd indulged in one another. "Time for us to get out of here." He narrowed his eyes in concern. "This won't get you into trouble, will it?"

Stepping back, she chuckled easily and waved her arm around. "I'm pretty sure *this* would get me into trouble. But if you're talking about my absence from my desk, then no. I often come and go when working on a story."

The minute she moved out of his embrace he missed her warmth and felt a little . . . lonely. He tried to keep his voice light. "Good. Let's get dressed." Sam gathered her clothes off the floor and handed them to her.

As he climbed into his jeans, Cat asked in a soft tone, "Why were you looking for me anyway?"

It took a moment for him to remember. Ah, the note. "I received a threatening letter from a protestor. Probably that same nut case that forced us to hide in here." He lowered his voice. "Of course, not that that was a bad thing."

Cat furrowed her brow. "A note?"

"Yeah, my Director has called in the police, but I thought maybe you could write another article or something to help clear this mess up."

She thinned her lips, anger brewing in her eyes. "I'm really sorry, Sam. I'll talk to my editor. I'll make this right for you. I promise. If Eugene had anything to do with this, I'll get to the bottom of it."

His heart turned over in his chest, loving the way she stood beside him, trying to do right by him after her article. "I take it Eugene was the protestor."

She nodded as her stomach growled. Sam chuckled and pulled his cell phone from his pocket.

Cat arched one perfect brow. "And you knew that was there all along?"

He grinned. "Yup. Now call someone to get us out of here so we can go back to my place to get something to eat."

"Your place?"

"Yeah, I'll make us something." It occurred to him a meal was just an excuse to keep her around longer. He enjoyed being with her, enjoyed their easy comfort and intimacy. "Come with me in my car and then I'll drive you back here tomorrow morning for work. I have to go right by here anyway."

A bemused expression crossed her face. "One question, Sam."

He shook his head in mock exasperation. "What's with you and all the questions anyway?"

She grinned. "I was just wondering if this meal requires oranges?" she asked. "I have a couple more on my desk."

Sam groaned. "Don't even get me started again, Cat, or we'll never get out of here."

Chapter 7

L ess than a half an hour later, after being rescued by maintenance and explaining in detail to Blain how she and Sam had managed to lock themselves in the storage room, Cat found herself sitting beside Sam in his Jeep. Of course, during her in-depth interrogation, she'd naturally left out the fine details of how they'd passed the hours while trapped inside said storage room.

Cat neatly folded her hands on her lap and studied Sam's profile as he maneuvered through mid-afternoon traffic. There was no denying that something had happened in that closet, something less physical, more emotional, and very intimate. Something that would be hard to walk away from when she moved to New York.

A riot of emotions swept through her and tugged on her heartstrings. She'd had no idea that Sam would come to mean so much to her in such a short time. But falling for him would only end up complicating her well-laid plans. Wouldn't it?

Cat turned in her seat, focusing all her attention on Sam. She concluded the tiny lines under his eyes were probably from worrying about Rio. A pang of guilt made her stomach tighten. God, she'd really had no idea her article would cause him such grief. She needed to make this right for him. No matter what it took.

Cat vowed to get to the bottom of this. If Eugene and Hawk were in cahoots, she'd find out. It was natural that Hawk would talk to Eugene for a follow-up, but Hawk had passed Eugene something and Cat was determined to find an explanation.

She opened her mouth, deciding Sam should know, and then changed her mind. He had enough to worry about without her adding to it, especially when she wasn't one hundred percent sure. If Sam took that information to the cops and Hawk proved innocent, it'd get her in a shitload of trouble at work. Then who'd ever hire her?

Redirecting her thoughts, Cat stifled a yawn and rested her head against the seat. Exhaustion eased itself into her bones. It had been one hell of an afternoon. And to think tomorrow night, she'd have a repeat performance while he tested her responses to the serum.

At the thought of tomorrow night her pulse rate kicked up

a notch. Another repeat performance from the skilled scientist would surely be her emotional undoing. She let out a long slow breath. How could she continue to be his lab rat and remain unscathed?

Sam pulled into his parking spot outside their condo, turned off the ignition, and shifted to face her. His eyes narrowed, his expression serious. "Are you okay?"

She nodded, feeling anything but. The way he looked at her with such tender concern made her throat tighten and heart ache. As she studied him, her chest hurt. Gut instinct told her to go home, run, lock the door, and never set eyes on Sam again. Entering into his territory, his personal space, and engaging in easy, playful banter over a casual meal would test the small brace holding the pieces of her heart together. She gazed into his Laguna blue eyes and felt herself drowning.

"How does grilled cheese sound? It's my specialty."

Apparently his culinary skills were right up there with hers. Cat gave an uneasy smile.

He must have sensed her hesitation. He didn't give her a chance to voice an argument. "Let me make you something to eat and then I'll walk you home," he pressed. The sexy lilt of his voice pulled at her, drawing her deeper into a dangerous place.

He smiled and that was all it took for her rational thought to pack up and take a vacation. One simple smoldering smile from him had her giving into temptation and going completely against her best interests.

Cat stretched out her body. Her muscles hurt. In all the right places. "Okay. My fridge is empty anyway."

Sam stepped from the Jeep and circled around to meet her. Gathering her hand in his he led her to his condo.

Suddenly, Sam stopped midstride. His mouth twisted into a frown. "Jesus, Cat. Two guys? At once?" He slipped his arm around her waist in a possessive manner and dragged her to him.

She felt his muscles bunch with tension. Tipping her chin, she took in the flare of anger in his eyes. "What are you talking about?"

He nodded toward her condo door.

Cat followed his gaze. "Oh." She waved. "Hey guys, over here."

As they came toward her, Sam widened his stance and tightened his hold on her. She heard him curse something incoherent under his breath.

"Sam, I'd like you to meet Mason and Luke."

Sam just stood there, legs wide, feet planted, staring at the two with a scowl on his face. Cat nudged him. "Don't be rude to my brothers."

Sam's head came up with a start. His face softened; his mood lightened. "Oh," he said, extending his hand. "Nice to meet you both. I didn't realize Cat had two brothers."

It occurred to her that Sam thought she was engaging in God knows what with two guys. At once! Like *she* was the one who was the local amusement ride.

"And we didn't realize she had a boyfriend," Mason said, assessing Sam.

Cat squared her shoulders. "That's because my private life is none of your business." She turned to Sam. "Sorry, Sam. Growing up the youngest girl with six older brothers hasn't been easy."

Sam smiled. "Six brothers?"

"Yeah, six brothers who come and go at all hours to check up on me." She turned to Mason and Luke, giving them a look that made them both take a measured step back. She loved her brothers with everything in her, but she just wished they'd give her a bit of breathing space. "Was there something you both wanted?"

Mason kicked at an imaginary stone. "Not really. I called a few times last night and you weren't home and Luke stopped by your paper today and you weren't there so we just thought we'd come by and see if everything was okay."

Exasperated, Cat shook her head and grinned. "I'm fine." She waved her hand at them. "Go home to your wives."

Sam clapped Mason on the back. "She's fine. Trust me. She's in good hands. I promise."

Cat shivered, remembering exactly how good those hands were. Leaning in, Cat gave her brothers a kiss on their cheeks and shooed them away. As they turned to leave, she grabbed Mason's elbow and said, "Give little Matt a hug for me and let him know I still have my rock. Tell Sarah I'll try to get by on the weekend."

As they moved away, Sam turned to her. "I like them," Sam said, sounding much happier than he had a few minutes ago.

"Good," she said, and wondered why that was so important to her.

As they continued on their way to Sam's condo, Cat wondered for a brief moment if she'd get a glimpse of his bedroom, to see if it looked any different from the inside. Sam unlocked his door, pushed it open, and gestured for her to enter. Always the gentleman, she mused.

She looked around, orienting herself. Familiarity hit. A replica of her place. Same layout. Same gray-colored carpet and off-white walls. Cat had planned to change the awful color just as soon as she found some spare time.

She tipped her head and glanced at Sam. "For a second there I thought I was home."

Sam shrugged off his coat, eased hers from her shoulders, and hung them in the entrance closet. The simple, domestic, normal, everyday act of him hanging her coat made her feel all weird inside.

He gestured with a wave. "Then I guess you already know where the kitchen is?"

Cat smiled and slipped off her shoes. Her feet were still killing her from her heels last night. She followed Sam down the short hallway. Her gaze journeyed to his ass. She brushed her tongue over her bottom lip and suppressed a growl of longing. Shame that her condo lacked that lovely master-piece.

He motioned toward the cluttered table. "Sorry about the mess, I would have cleaned up if I had known you were coming over."

"It doesn't look any different from my place. I like to think of it as organized clutter."

Sam chuckled. "I've never quite heard it put that way before. Just push the stuff out of your way and grab a seat. Would you like a coffee or tea?"

"I'd love a tea, thanks." Cat gathered the newspapers from the chair and table and neatly piled them while Sam filled the kettle and then made a quick trip to the bathroom to wash up. A stack of cutout articles caught her attention. She reached for them. Her breath stalled as she flipped through the pieces. She spent a long moment just staring at them. Sam returned from washing up and grabbed the cheese slices from the fridge.

She worked to recover her voice. "Sam?"

Sam placed the frying pan on the stove and turned to face her. "What's up?"

She fanned the articles in the air. "You read my articles?"

He folded his arms and leaned against his countertop. "Yeah."

Surprise registered on her face. Her voice rose a notch. "And you cut them out and keep them?" she asked, wrinkling her nose.

Sam pushed off from the counter, took two steps toward her, and brushed her hair from her face. His soft caress, so tender and gentle, made her knees wobble. Sam dipped his head, his voice softened. "Is that so hard to believe?"

She shrugged and lowered her eyes. "I . . . I . . . it just surprises me is all."

"Well, you shouldn't be surprised. Your articles are great, Cat. Worth a second read." He cupped her chin and lifted her gaze to his.

She opened her eyes wide and met his glance. "You really like them?"

Sam rolled one shoulder. "Sure. Everyone at work does too." He rifled through them. "This one here about a guy's quick trip to the E.R. after his girlfriend turned him into a banana split and mistakenly chomped down on the wrong banana is my favorite. Someone read this one out loud in the lunchroom. It had us laughing all day."

She lowered herself into the chair, furrowed her brow, and tossed him a skeptical look. "Really?"

He threw his hands up. "Yes, Cat. Really. Why do you find that so hard to believe?"

She stammered. "I don't know. I knew they were popular but they're just fluff pieces." She rotated her ankles and rubbed the pad of her thumb over her heel. Sam sat across from her, gathered her feet, and took over the massage.

Cat shimmied lower in her seat. "Mmmm . . . feels good. Thanks."

His voice had taken on a serious edge. His lips thinned. "Cat, do you enjoy writing these articles?"

She smiled, then hesitated before answering. "I do. It's just that I want to write something important, something that matters."

A frown furrowed his brow. He grabbed a stack of papers and plunked them down in front of her. He flipped open a page. "Tell me what you see."

She raised an inquisitive brow. "What are you doing?"

"Just tell me. What do you see?" he pressed.

"I see news articles."

"About what?"

Cat leaned in closer, squinted, and read the first caption. "Murder."

Sam flipped a page. "And here, what do you see?"

"Drug bust."

He pointed to another caption farther down the page. "And here?"

"Political scandal." She sighed and leaned back. "What's your point?"

He shook his head and tossed her a perplexed frown. "This is what you want to write? This is what you consider important?"

"I just want to make a difference."

He raked his hair from his forehead, obviously frustrated. "Don't you see? You do make a difference. Your amusing articles take the sting out of everyday life. They remind us how to smile. That not everything in life is bad." He waved his hand toward the paper. "Don't undervalue yourself. What you do is as important, if not more important, than what these other journalists do. You brighten up our days."

Shocked.

A description befitting her current emotion. Shocked and touched, actually. She'd had no idea that Sam had such respect for her work. She opened her mouth but no words formed.

The whistling kettle drew Sam's attention. She watched as he stood, gently placed her feet on his chair, and went about preparing her tea.

She'd never considered her work important before. She always equated success with writing hard-hitting news, at least that's what had always been pounded into her by her parents.

Was Sam right? Was she undervaluing herself? Was she already a success and just hadn't realized it? She had to admit, she loved writing those humorous pieces, loved meeting new people, and hearing their dating and mating woes.

Sam came back with the hot drink. "I understand that drive to succeed, Cat. I have that same drive myself. This project I'm working on has consumed me for the last six months. Believe me, I'm not undermining what you think is important. But I think you're missing something. You're already a success." He spread his arms wide to emphasize the point. "A huge success."

She lowered her voice. "Thank you, Sam." Her heart turned over in her chest as she took a moment to let his words sink in. To reevaluate things.

She lowered her head and spoke into her cup. "It was my father's dream to see me follow in his footsteps. After he died, it pushed me that much harder. I wanted to make him proud of me."

Sam touched her hand and squeezed. "I'm sorry, Cat. But I do think he would be proud of you. Proud to know how wonderful your columns are, how many people they touch."

Cat swallowed the lump in her throat. Had she been chasing the wrong dream all along? Had it taken Sam York to make her see that? Or had she really known that all along.

She glanced at him. "Did you always want to be a scientist?" She sipped her tea and studied his expression.

His low chuckle curled around her and seeped beneath her skin. "For as long as I can remember, I was always doing some kind of experiment in the basement. I've blown up a few things in my day. The fire department knew me much better than they should have." He picked her feet up and eased them back onto his lap.

Ticklish, she wiggled her toes as he resumed his massage. She smiled as the image of a young, geeky, scientific Sam rushed through her mind. "I bet your mom loved that."

He frowned. She could feel tension rising in him. "I wouldn't know. It was just me and my dad. When something bigger and better came along my mom bailed."

"Bigger and better?" Cat's heart stalled, recalling how her father had always used those same words.

"Yeah, a better job, a better husband, a bigger house, and a bigger bank account. After my mom left, my father had plenty of different women coming and going. It was the same with them too. They left when bigger and better came along."

She reached out and touched his hand, her heart twisting in her chest. She felt so close to him at that moment. Something told her he'd just opened up and shared a private, painful side of him that he'd never shared before.

"I'm sorry, Sam."

He shrugged and stood. "It doesn't matter anymore. It was a long time ago."

It may have been a long time ago, but Cat suspected it had a profound impact on his life and his lifestyle. Was this the reason Sam played the field, a different woman every week? Was he afraid to get too close only to have a woman leave him after he offered his heart?

Over the last few days Cat had caught glimpses of the true Sam. She could see beneath that playboy façade. He was giving, nurturing, caring, and so very, very vulnerable.

Cat's stomach took that moment to grumble. Sam smiled. "I'd better feed you before you pass out on me."

"Can I help?"

"Nope, just enjoy your tea."

"Sounds good to me," she said, stretching out.

Sam chuckled.

"Actually, I need to wash up, too. Can I use your bathroom?"

He waved his spatula toward the hall. "Sure, you know where it is."

Cat stood, pushed up on her tiptoes, and pressed a kiss to Sam's cheek, needing almost desperately to make an intimate connection.

He seemed shocked by the gesture. He gripped the sides of her hips. "What was that for?"

One shoulder rolled. "For being so sweet."

He gruffed, "Sweet? I'm not sweet. I'm badass. You must have me confused with someone else."

Cat lowered her voice. "There is no one else, Sam."

Something in his expression changed. His eyes softened, his hand touched her cheek and traced the pattern of her face. "Go wash up, this will just take a second." She was astonished by the tenderness in his voice.

She gave a tight nod, twisted around to leave, and felt his eyes on her as she rounded the corner. As she made her way to the bathroom, she glanced at the walls and noted all the baby pictures. "Are these pictures of you, Sam?"

"No, they're my goddaughter." She heard the love in his voice.

Cat felt her heart tighten. Sam had a goddaughter and plastered pictures of her all over his walls. Well, that simply confirmed it; there was way more to this man than met the eye.

Cat closed the bathroom door and washed up. When she stepped back into the hall, she took another moment to look at the pictures of the beautiful baby girl. She wondered if Sam wanted kids.

"What's her name?"

"Samantha, after me." She could hear the pride in his voice.

"She's beautiful." Cat stepped back into the kitchen as Sam placed her sandwich on the table.

"I'm babysitting her this weekend. Maybe you can stop by."

Cat saw the love and longing shining in his eyes. Her stomach rolled, but not from hunger. "I'd like that." Her own voice was rough with emotion.

Turning her attention to her sandwich, she bit into it. Trying for casual she said, "This is delicious."

"Good," Sam said.

"I'd have to say this is the best grilled cheese I've ever had." She grinned and added with a wink. "Probably because I didn't have to make it."

Sam chuckled and sat beside her, taking a bite out of his own sandwich.

Cat glanced around. "Where's Rio."

"At the lab. After I drop you off, I'll go get her. Sometimes I leave her at the lab, but I'd feel better if she's with me tonight."

A few minutes later, after their sandwiches were gone, Cat sat back, stretched, and gave a contented sigh. She glanced at the clock, knowing she should go, but not wanting the day to end.

"I should probably go. It's getting late and you need to go get Rio."

"And we still have a lot of work ahead of us tomorrow night," he reminded her. "Come on. I'll walk you to your door."

As she walked by another stack of pictures of Samantha on her way to the door, she thought of her nephew Matt, and how much she loved to snuggle and play with him. How much joy and love he brought into her life.

She felt Sam's hand close over hers. When his thumb softly brushed her skin in a warm caress, she wondered, for the first time in ages, what *she* really wanted in life. She'd been living her father's dream for so long she'd forgotten what her own dreams were, what made her happy.

She swallowed, needing time alone to sort through her feelings. "I'm fine, Sam. It's just across the courtyard."

He ignored her protest and followed her to his door.

She rolled her eyes. "You're worse than my brothers."

He dipped his head. His hair fell forward and she didn't even hesitate to push it off his forehead. "I promised them you were in good hands, and I don't break my promises." When she gazed into his eyes, she knew there was a new closeness between them. She felt it in every fiber of her being.

Like the true gentleman he was, he helped her with her coat, circled his arm around her shoulder, and hastily walked her across the dimly lit courtyard.

Standing outside her condo, she crimped her neck to look at him. Warmth settled in her stomach. "Thanks, Sam." Turning around, she inserted her key into the lock and pushed open her door. "I'll see you in the morning then," she said, remembering she'd left her car at the office.

Sam cupped her elbow and urged her back. His roped muscles tightened. "Cat. I was wondering," he said, his voice a gruff whisper.

She twisted to face him. Dear God, when his deep blue eyes looked directly at her like that, it was possible to forget every sane thought. He tucked her hair behind her ear. A grin curled his mouth as he inched forward. His sensuous lips were so close she could almost taste them.

She squared her shoulders, her spine starched. "What is it?"

His rich baritone licked over her thighs. A muscle in his jaw twitched. "Should I leave my blinds open tonight?"

She froze. Her mouth opened in a silent gasp. Holy hell, he knew. All this time, he knew she'd been secretly watching him in his bedroom. She bit back an agonized groan.

His eyes were full of teasing warmth as they moved over her. His smile brimming with tenderness. "Or have you had your fill of me?"

"I . . . I . . ."

He leaned in and pressed his ear against hers. "Why don't you leave yours open, too," he said, his voice full of tortured promise. "After I get back from picking up Rio, I'll meet you at the window."

Less than an hour later, Sam pulled into the parking lot, Rio in tow. With long, hurried strides, Sam rushed to his condo, all the while wondering if Cat would indeed play his little voyeur game. His cock thickened as a wave of anticipation took hold.

Of course, he knew she watched him at night. Hell, he had to be watching her to know she watched him. On many nights he'd purposely left his blinds open, hoping to get a glimpse of the sexy woman across the courtyard. The sight of her always played havoc on his senses. Once her lights dimmed, he'd retreat to his own bed and imagine there wasn't a courtyard separating them.

He pushed past his condo door and locked it behind him. After securing his tired chimp in her bed, he rushed to his bedroom. Sam opened his blinds and peered into Cat's window. Her outside light cast mysterious patterns on her walls. He took a moment to reminisce about the way her body had opened up to him this afternoon. He could still hear her sweet voice in his head. Calling out his name, begging for him to take her where she needed to go.

Desire moved over and through him as he recalled the way she'd burned up in his arms when he'd slid his tongue over her trembling flesh. The way she had eagerly responded to his touch and his kisses had made him mad with longing. The way her eyes had churned with emotions, and blazed with hunger, had taken him to a foreign place where no coherent thought existed. It was unnerving the way he'd lost control and had become completely consumed by her. He suspected being with Cat had changed the fate of his future forever.

Cat moved to her window. Sam shifted his stance. A half smile turned up his lips when he caught sight of her gorgeous body silhouetted in the dark. Damn, he loved her sense of adventure.

He studied the contours of the woman he now knew intimately. His heart leapt as a sense of longing tugged at him and ripped a hole in the shield around his heart. He couldn't understand his reactions to her. He'd never experienced such a yearning before. Nor had he ever opened up to anyone and told them about his past. What in the hell had possessed him to do that?

Sam peeled off his shirt as Cat slowly, seductively unbuttoned her blouse. He licked his lips and scrubbed a hand over his chin, recalling the texture and taste of those hard-marbled nipples. He could almost feel her warm breath caressing his bare skin. Without taking his eyes from her, he pulled off his pants and kicked them away.

Once again, his body grew needy for her. The oddest sensations settled in his gut. Something about her pulled at him. Cat Nichols was quickly becoming his weakness. The truth penetrated his defenses as a riot of emotions rushed through him.

Cat stretched out her arms, slipped her finger between her wet lips and then touched herself, rubbing her moistened fingertip over her dark nipples. The sweet torture made him throb.

Completely rattled, Sam swallowed. His heart rate galloped. *Sweet Mother of God.* She was going to pay for that tomorrow night. Using his tongue, he planned on parting her folds, dipping into her sweet spot, branding her plump clit with his heat, stroking, lapping, bringing her higher and higher, driving her as crazy as she was driving him right now.

He felt his composure slip away. No longer able to fight the inevitable, his hand went to his throbbing dick. He growled. His blood flowed hot through his veins. His nostrils flared as his fingers closed around his thickness.

Her hand slid lower over her body. She traced the pattern of her curves until her fingers disappeared below the window pane. He could only imagine she was playing with her sweet spot.

Lord, he hungered to touch her there again, to taste her. He also hungered for her touch. Wanted her hands all over his body, claiming him as her own, branding him.

Being with her was so easy, so comfortable. So natural. Warmth streaked through him. His heart clenched, knowing where his thoughts were taking him, knowing he was venturing into unknown territory. When he wasn't paying attention, she'd slipped beneath his skin without even trying. Cat Nichols was different from every other woman he'd been with. She'd taken him to a place where he'd never let himself go before. Taking him to a deeper level of intimacy where emotions ruled his actions.

He'd never had a relationship last past a few months. Never wanted to. Over the last twenty-four hours something had changed because suddenly he was thinking just that.

Hell, he wanted her.

For himself.

A wave of possessiveness swamped him at the thoughts of her becoming intimate with another man. A quick flash of anger made his blood boil. He swiped away the moisture collecting on his forehead and cursed under his breath.

He watched Cat's hand slide back up her body. She lifted her fingers in the air, gave a little wave, and blew him a goodnight kiss. A moment later she backed away from the window, out of his line of vision.

As he watched her go, his heart churned for something more, something deeper, something forever.

She was a journalist, climbing her way to the top. What if he opened himself up to her and took a chance on what was between them, only to have her bail when something bigger and better came along?

What if she didn't?

Chapter 8

C at's morning had passed by in a flurry of activity. After she'd engaged in easy conversation with Sam during her ride to work, he'd dropped her off outside her building as promised. Cat had worked furiously to finish her article and make her deadline.

Now she sat there, toying with her pencil, impatiently waiting for Blain to finish his conference call so she could once again pester him about clearing things up for Sam.

Cat didn't trust Hawk enough to believe he'd make things right. And after spotting him with that protestor yesterday, she suspected he was up to no good. As soon as she had proof, she'd take it to Blain.

Just before her noon hour break, Blaine had poked his head out of his office. "Cat, can I see you in here for a minute?"

She climbed from her chair. "Sure, what's up?" Her mind raced, wondering if he'd wanted to interrogate her again about the supply closet incident. Or maybe he'd changed his mind about the article. Yeah, and maybe Hawk would take to the sky and fly away, never to be heard from again.

"Have a seat." Blain motioned to a chair across from his desk as he made his way to his own seat. "Rumor has it you've applied at the *Daily Press* in New York."

Well, he certainly got right to the point.

She rolled her shoulder. "Rumor is right."

Blain scrubbed his hand over his chin and she noted the tired lines bracketing his eyes. "I don't want to lose you, Cat. In fact, I'm hoping what I have to tell you will entice you to stay."

She raised an inquisitive brow. "Go on."

"I've been working on this for awhile. I didn't want to mention it until I had confirmation. Your column was just picked up for national syndication."

Her eyes flew open. "No way!"

Blain laughed. "Cat, it's not that I don't think you're good enough for hard-hitting news. I do. It's just that your talent and personality are better suited for your humorous 'Cat on the Prowl' columns. People love them. They're eating them up like sugar-coated candy."

Cat got quiet for a moment as she mulled over the news. Her thoughts strayed to her parents. Warmth curled around her as she reflected on what Sam had said to her the night before. Deep in her heart she knew her mother and father would be proud of her and would want her to choose a path that made her happy.

She glanced up to see Blain watching her, his brow furrowed in concentration as he gauged her reactions. "You can let me know at the end of the week, okay?"

Nodding, Cat stood. "Thanks, Blain. One more thing."

He rolled his eyes, but his smile was genuine. "I'll see to it that Hawk does a proper follow-up on the story. And make sure he gets his facts right," he said with a wink.

Cat planted her hands on her hips. "If he doesn't, I'm writing another article," she said, challenging him.

Blain laughed. "Stick to what you do best, Cat."

Cat smiled, touched that he had so much faith in her, and fought to keep her as an employee. "Thank you," she said, and made her way back to her desk.

After Cat returned a dozen phone calls from people wanting to be interviewed for her article, she climbed from her chair and stretched. She glanced at her watch and noted that time had gotten away from her. She needed to get home to prepare for tonight's experiment.

A half an hour later Cat changed lanes and maneuvered her car through dinner hour traffic. The dashboard clock indicated that she had less than an hour to get ready before Sam picked her up to help him complete his research. She switched lanes again after the traffic in front of her came to a complete standstill.

She hadn't expected to be running so late or to be caught in rush hour traffic. Cripes, she felt like she was stuck smack dab in the middle of a freaking snail convention.

Tapping her fingers impatiently on her dashboard, Cat flicked on the radio and waited. Finally, traffic began moving again. A short while later Cat tapped her brakes and eased into her exit. As she neared her condo, her thoughts returned to Sam. They always returned to Sam. Even when she wasn't with him, he was always with her. In her mind. Under her skin.

Once this project was complete and he got what he *needed* from her, would he resume his "Romeo" lifestyle—as Jen had described it? Would she stand in her window and watch a bevy of women come and go from his condo? Her stomach lurched. She felt physically ill. She could no longer pretend it didn't matter.

Cat pulled into her driveway and rushed inside her condo. Her stomach grumbled as she kicked off her shoes and sifted through her mail. She'd be lucky to grab a quick bite before Sam arrived. Stepping farther into her condo, she stripped off her jacket and tossed it onto the sofa.

The doorbell chimed.

She stopped dead in her tracks. Sam couldn't be here this early, could he? Cat padded across the floor, peeked through the peephole, and then pulled the door open. She came face-to-face with her grinning friend.

"Hey Jen, I'm kind of in a hurry," she rushed out, unbuttoning her silk top, needing to get a quick shower before Sam showed up.

"Well, how was it?"

Cat crinkled her nose and pinned her friend with a glare. "Have you ever known me to kiss and tell?"

Jen chuckled. "So there was kissing involved, was there?" she probed, stepping inside the condo, shutting the door behind her.

Cat pulled her top off and walked to the kitchen. She called over her shoulder, "I have to get a shower before Sam gets here. We have more research to do tonight." Opening the fridge she popped a strawberry into her mouth, attempting to appease her hunger.

Keeping pace, Jen followed behind. "*Research?* That's what they call it these days, is it?" she teased. She leaned against the doorjamb while Cat rifled through her produce drawer.

"I thought you might want this," Jen said.

Cat peeked over the top of the door to see Jen hold out an envelope. A wide smile split her pretty face. "It's from the *Daily Press*. It landed in my mail slot by mistake."

Cat's heart stilled. The refrigerator door slipped shut as she came out from behind it. "You're kidding," she said around a mouthful of strawberry. "I just sent my resume off a week ago. I didn't expect to hear from them so soon." She wiped juice from her lips, accepted the envelope, and plopped herself into a wooden chair.

Jen lowered herself into the chair opposite her, her eyes wide in anticipation. Cat ripped open the envelope and scanned the letter. She read it once, let out a heavy breath, and read it a second time, assessing the information.

"Bad news?"

Cat tipped her head. "Well, not really. They're interested in my work."

"Whoo hoo! That's great, Cat." Jen paused and narrowed her eyes. "Hold on, what's up with you? This is what you want. What you've always wanted. You should be up doing the River Dance. Why aren't you?"

"It seems my article on the Iowa Research Center really intrigued them. So much so, they want me to fly to New York for a personal interview." She twisted her lips and furrowed her brow.

Jen's eyes opened wide. "And you have a problem with this? Why?"

Cat dropped the letter on the table and pinched the bridge of her nose. "It's not as simple as that."

One brow rose, intrigued. "No?"

"My editor just told me my column was going into national syndication."

"Really, that's fabulous Cat. But isn't this the break you've been waiting for? I once remember you saying you'd do anything to write hard-hitting news for the *Daily Press*. What has changed?"

Everything.

"I thought you wanted to break away from writing what you consider *fluff* articles? Even though I think they're fabulous."

Cat swallowed. "So does Sam and the rest of the world apparently."

Jen sat back, bobbed her head, tapped her fingers on the table, and tossed her a knowing smile.

"What?" Cat asked defensively, bracing herself for more of Jen's textbook psychology.

"It's Sam, isn't it? You got it bad for him."

When Cat didn't respond, Jen blew out a breath and continued. "Dammit Cat. You've had it bad for him for months, haven't you? Is that why you haven't been dating anyone?"

She shook her head adamantly. "No, there are just no good guys out there." It was a half-truth.

"And you think Sam is one of the good ones?"

Cat rolled her shoulders. "Maybe."

Jen nodded to the envelope. "I thought this was your dream."

Cat gave a wan smile. "I think I might have been chasing

the wrong dream. I think everything I want is right here. It has been all along and I just didn't realize it."

Jen's features softened. "Does Sam feel the same way about you?"

"I don't know."

"Then maybe it's time for you to find out if he thinks of you as more than his lab rat."

Cat nodded, knowing exactly what she had to do. After their experiment tonight she'd invite Sam back here and tell him about the job offer. To see if it mattered to him. To see if he'd ask her to stay. She needed to find out if she meant more to him than a sex experiment.

Sam paced around his apartment, watching the clock, counting the hours until he could pick up Cat. As he moved through his condo, he stopped for a moment to look at the pictures of Samantha. A surge of love rushed to his heart. His gaze traveled to Erin and Kale's wedding picture. As he took in the vision, envy hit him hard and nearly knocked him to his knees.

His jaw clenched. His heart pounded. And he couldn't deny it any longer.

He wanted that. He *longed* for that. All of that. The wife, the kids, the love, the trust, and the comfort. And he wanted it with Cat. She'd broken through his barriers, touched him down deep, and brought warmth to his darkest corners.

He was tired of being a coward. Afraid to put himself out there. Afraid of getting hurt. He was tired of being alone . . . of being lonely. Tired of looking in from the outside, watching and wishing he had a family of his own.

He'd gotten more than he'd bargained for when he agreed to Cat's plan, allowing her to step in for his lab rat so he could salvage his project. During his experiment he'd totally lost himself in her . . . body and soul. How could he not, really? She was loving, caring, and perfect in every way, and he'd gone and fallen in love with her. And maybe . . . just maybe with the good Lord willing, he had what it took to keep her around.

Feeling edgy and restless, Sam paced. Perspiration dotted his forehead as he clenched and unclenched his fists, sorting through things with his mind.

He wanted Cat. Forever.

Deep in his gut he knew that living without her wasn't living at all.

So what the hell was he going to do about it?

Worry rushed through him. He drew a shaky breath. What if she didn't feel the same way?

What if she did?

It was time for him to step out of his comfort zone, push past his fears, and find out if they could have a future together.

Sam glanced at the clock and knew he was early, but he

had to go to her. He jogged the short distance between their condos and lifted his hand to knock when the door suddenly opened. A surprised Jen stood there.

"Hi." He looked past her shoulder. "Is Cat here?"

Jen nodded. "She's in the shower." She opened the door wider and gestured for him to enter. "She asked me to lock up on my way out, so will you do that for me?"

"Sure."

Sam shut the door and set the lock. He listened to the rush of water as he made his way down the hall. With the bathroom door ajar he could see her reflection in the mirror. His body reacted with urgent demands and his heart filled with emotions at the mere sight of her. Everything in him screamed possession, urging him to scoop her up, carry her away, and keep her to himself forever. He closed his eyes briefly. The depth of his desire for her completely threw him. No one had ever rocked his world like Cat Nichols.

The water turned off. Cat pulled back her clear plastic curtain and draped a towel around her body. Feeling like a kid caught with his hand in the cookie jar, Sam took a couple of steps back.

"Jen, is that you? I thought you'd already left."

He cleared his throat and called out to her. "It's me."

"Oh?" He heard a rustle before she joined him in the hall. A single white towel knotted around her breasts was the only thing keeping his eyes from devouring her gorgeous body.

Her cheeks were flushed from the hot water, her wet hair clung to her shoulders and back. Water droplets dripped down her neck and soaked into the plush towel.

"Sam, how did you get in?" Cat glanced down the hall, searching for Jen.

"Jen let me in and then left."

Cat nodded in understanding, wiped water from her face, and blinked her beautiful green eyes. "You're early."

It took entirely too much work to keep his glance from traveling down to examine her long, sleek, sexy legs. "I wanted to catch you before you ate dinner."

Cat smiled. "Dinner sounds fabulous. I'm starving."

Dinner was an excuse and he damn well knew it. He wanted to spend every waking second with her. He produced a vial with the serum. "The serum is supposed to increase all senses, including taste, so I thought we'd test that at the same time." It was a small lie, but he needed to see how she felt before he blurted out his feelings and told her exactly how much he wanted her. This was all so new to him.

"Of course. Just give me a minute to get ready and then I'll take it."

Chapter 9

L ess than a half an hour later Sam escorted Cat to the research room. He pushed open the door to let her in. "How are you feeling?" Narrowing his eyes, he examined her.

Cat held out her hand. "Shaky from hunger. I thought we were going to grab a bite to eat."

"We are." He nodded to the center of the room.

Cat glanced at the dinner table. It was beautifully set for two. She smiled. "Once again you surprise me with the details, Sam. Everything looks great."

His chest puffed up, clearly thrilled by her approval and appreciation. "That's because you deserve only the best." Her smile widened and made his heart rise to his throat. "Come on. Let's eat before you pass out on me."

They sat across from one another at a table full of fresh fruit, cheese, and breads.

Sam cocked a brow. "Champagne?"

"I'd love some." Cat grabbed a plump red grape and popped it in her mouth. She licked her lips and moaned a sweet sexy bedroom moan. Sam watched, captivated. The thoughts of popping something else between those luscious lips made his body vibrate, nearly causing him to spill the damn champagne. After he managed to pour two glasses, he handed her one.

Cat took a small sip and crinkled her nose. "The bubbles tickle." She reached for a piece of cheese and bread and nibbled them. "God, everything tastes so good."

Sam smiled, picked up a strawberry, and put it in her mouth. She moaned in delight, taking great pleasure in her food. Watching her made him wild with the need to make love to her, to push inside her tight sheath and remain there forever.

"It's the enhancer, Cat." His voice dropped to a whisper. "It's already beginning to heighten your senses." Not to mention his own.

She shrugged and wiggled in her chair. "Maybe it's just because I'm starving." She opened her mouth, inviting him to feed her. "More." There was a note of amusement in her sweet voice.

Sam shifted his chair closer, until his legs pressed against hers. Heat flared between them as their thighs collided. He reached out and stroked her cheek. Using small circular motions he brushed the pad of his thumb over her skin, all the while his body language indicating that he was imagining it was another part of her body he was caressing. Her eyes blazed with desire as they locked with his.

He brought a slice of fresh orange to her mouth and held it just out of her reach.

She whimpered, flicked her tongue out, and drew it into her mouth. Eyes closed, her head lolled to the side. A sigh of pleasure filled the room. The erotic vision before him fueled his desire, causing his body to go up in flames.

He had to taste, to have her, to make love to her and have her want him on the same emotional level.

His lips crashed down on hers. Her lids flew open. She gasped in surprise. He drew her orange-soaked tongue into his mouth for a more thorough taste. She leaned into him, deepening the kiss, pressing her lips hungrily into his. Urgent hands moved over her curves, unable to get enough of her. Unable to get her deep enough under his skin.

"Sam," she whispered through muffled kisses.

"Yeah?"

She inched back, her smile coy, the gleam in her eyes turning wicked. "I know a better way to test my sense of taste." Unbridled desire laced her voice.

He felt so crazed with lust, desire, and need he couldn't comprehend what she was trying to tell him.

"What are you talking about?"

"I think I want to kiss you."

"Cat. We are kissing."

She shook her head. "Not there." Cat stood, pushed her chair away and positioned herself between his open thighs.

He gulped and began trembling from head to toe as her glance traveled down his body and settled on his cock.

"What are you doing, Cat?"

"Well, I've been dying to taste you again since yesterday, so I thought we could test my sense of taste this way."

"Test your what?" he asked, confused.

She chuckled. "The experiment, Sam. The serum. My heightened senses."

"Right," he forced that one word out and nodded in agreement, knowing his need to be with her had nothing to do with the experiment.

Her movements were sensual, seductive as she dropped to her knees, leaned back on her heels, and worked his jeans past his legs. With her mouth only inches from his cock, she blew out a breath. His engorged phallus jolted in anticipation as the heat of her breath whispered over his thighs. She sheathed his hard cock in her hand, her fingers idly stroking, the same way one would caress a pet.

As she licked her lips, he made quick work of his shirt. "Very impressive, Sam. I should have told you that yesterday."

A rumble of pleasure sounded low in his throat. He could feel her hot mouth so close to his cock. Man, it felt so damn good. He jerked his hips forward, his dick brushing her lips.

"Oh God, Cat." He took short, panting breaths.

His juices pearled on the top. Her long golden locks fell forward, shadowing her face as she dipped her head. Her tongue slid over his engorged tip, tasting his essence. The silky sweep of her lashes against his skin made him throb. His body tightened and he nearly shot off in her mouth.

She breathed a kiss over his flesh, taking great pleasure in his size and texture. He took deep fortifying breaths and gathered her hair in his palms, pulling it from her face as she slowly drew the length of him into her throat. Her pretty pink tongue swirled around his head, pushing him to the edge of oblivion. Fire pitched through him, sending his blood pressure soaring.

Sweat trickled down his neck as he became lost in the pleasure of her expert mouth. Her velvet tongue worked harder as she switched tactics. Small, urgent, short flicks around his tip evolved into long determined strokes down his length.

Her tongue played around his heavy sac, forcing it to draw tight inside his body as pleasure forked through him. She pulled one ball into her mouth and suckled, drawing an orgasm from his dick. Sweet Jesus, that was all he could take.

He gripped her head to ease her off his cock. He was going to come.

"Cat . . ." he growled between clenched teeth. His muscles began to clench. "Cat . . . the bed . . . now. I want to be inside you when I come."

She glanced up at him, her gaze revealing her every emotion. When their glances met something special, unique passed between them. The warmth and emotion in her eyes spoke volumes. She felt the same way about him.

He felt a tug in his gut.

Maybe it was higher.

And a little to the left.

He lowered his voice. "Sweetheart, let me make love to you on the bed."

Cat smiled up at him and gave an erotic whimper. Her soft feminine features pulled at his heart as a bolt of emotionally charged energy arced between them.

She glanced at the bed. "I've never had sex on silk sheets before."

His jaw slackened open, clearly appalled. "Then Cat, my love, you haven't been treated properly. Tonight I'm going to rectify that."

Sam was right. No man had ever treated her so properly. Not only did Sam care about her pleasures, but he was eager for them as well. Her heart tightened in her chest as she met his glance. She gazed deep into his eyes and met longing. There was something different in the way he looked at her. Was it possible he saw her as something more than a lab rat?

She stood, took a small step back, and removed her clothes. Gaze riveted, Sam's mouth curved enticingly as he watched her step from her jeans and slowly inch down her panties. She shivered as a chill prowled through her.

"Cat . . ." His soft voice pulled her in. "I want you so much."

Sam made a swift move and put his arms around her, firing her blood. She shimmied closer, tangled her arms around his neck, and locked her legs around his hips as he picked her up and carried her to the bed, sprawling her across a splash of silk sheets.

The silk felt cool against her heated flesh. He leaned over her. His gaze held her captive as he pressed his lips over hers. His kiss was full of passion, tenderness, emotion. "I need to taste you again, Cat."

Her heart pounded and her breath stalled. Her pussy muscles began to undulate and clench at his promising words.

Positioning himself between her spread legs, he leaned in close. With a feathery light caress he pulled open her swollen folds. She shuddered as he inhaled her aroused scent.

He looked at her with such desire she thought she'd melt all over the sheets. "You're beautiful," he whispered, his voice harsh, rough. He pushed one finger inside her drenched pussy, the pad of his thumb nudging her clitoris. Rhythmically, he eased in and out of her quivering channel. She moaned and pitched forward.

He growled at her responsiveness. "Your responses make me wild."

He pulled his finger all the way out, cupped her backside, and lifted her ass off the bed. He brought his mouth close to her pussy and inhaled. His nostrils flared. "You smell so good." His warm breath heated her nether lips to the boiling point.

"Please, Sam . . ." she begged. With that he answered her urgent plea and sank his mouth into her heat, feasting on her.

She arched right off the bed. "Oh Sam!"

"You are so hot, Cat."

The room began to spin as Sam seared her clit with his tongue. His fingers moved back inside her needy fissure to play with her oversensitized G-spot. Her head whipped to the side; her throat went dry. She licked her lips and took deep gulping breaths as the pressure of an orgasm mounted.

"Come for me, baby. Let me taste you again."

His words, his voice, and the tenderness in his eyes pushed her over the edge. He sucked harder on her clit, drawing it into his mouth, playing with it.

She opened her mouth in a silent gasp as stars danced before her eyes. She thrust forward; her body convulsed.

Powerful emotions surged through her as a wave of liquid heat rushed to his mouth. Every nerve in her body vibrated and burned from sensory overload, but she couldn't tell whether it was from the serum or from being with the man she loved.

He climbed up her body and lightly, lovingly brushed his lips over hers. He grabbed a condom from the side table and slipped it on. Nestling back between her legs, his cock probed her opening as his gaze bore into the depths of her soul. He brushed her hair from her face. Her heart jumped. His intimate touch was different. Less physical, more emotional.

She touched his cheek, her need for him completely overwhelming her. "Sam, make love to me."

"My pleasure." He closed his mouth over hers, swallowing her gasp as he plunged into her. She held him tight, hugging him as his lovemaking stirred all her emotions. God, he felt so wonderful. She'd never experienced such raw, intense need in her life.

He pumped, she arched, and all rational thought dissolved. Balancing on his arms, his muscles tightened and flexed. Together they established a rhythm. His heat reached out to her, curling around her, warming her from the inside out.

His voice was low, rough. "You are so hot and tight, Cat. I won't last."

"I'm already there again, Sam," she whispered, running her fingers though his hair, pulling, tugging, needing all of him, yet not able to get him close enough.

She drew him to her. "Hold me." He slipped his arms under her shoulders and pressed his chest against hers as another orgasm washed over her.

Their bodies fused as one as her sex muscles clenched around his cock. "Baby, I feel your hot juices." Sam thrust harder, driving her deeper into the mattress. "Oh God, Cat." His cock pulsed and throbbed in the depths of her core as he came inside her channel.

He rolled onto his side. Never breaking contact, he brought her with him. She cuddled into a wall of muscle and felt the rapid rise and fall of his chest. He stroked her cheek, brushing her hair from her forehead. When he touched her like that, like he really meant it, her world turned upside down.

They held each other for a long moment, as if their very lives depended on it. Without even thinking about it their fingers searched each other out and linked together.

She drew a deep breath and said calmly, "Sam, I think we have a problem."

"A problem?"

She shook her head. "You see, I was so busy making love to you, I forgot to gauge my responses."

"That's not good, Cat."

"Nope, not good at all."

"What does that mean?" he questioned in a soft tone.

She frowned. "I'm afraid I'm going to have to run the experiment again."

He shook his head in mock exasperation. "Where are you ever going to find another stud like me at this time of night?"

Cat couldn't help but to smile. "It's impossible. So that really only leaves one solution."

"Only one?" he asked, no longer able to keep the grin from his handsome face.

"Only one." She crushed her body against his, her hard nipples giving him a silent message.

He blew out an exaggerated breath. "Well hell, the things I have to do in the name of science."

Chapter *10*

They were both quiet, lost in their own thoughts during the ride back to their condo complex. Sam took that time to reflect on the night's events and the emotions Cat had pulled from him. He cradled her hand in his, needing the physical contact at all times.

He parked his vehicle and turned in his seat. His heart galloped as he gazed at her. He couldn't let this night end. Not yet. Not ever. He needed to be around her. To spend the night. To fall asleep locked in each other's embrace. He gently stroked her face, wanting to tell her how he felt but needing to hear her say it first.

"Nightcap?" His voice was rough with emotions.

"Yes, my place." She said it quickly as though she'd been considering it for quite some time.

Moonlight spilled over their bodies as they crossed the

parking lot. As they made their way to Cat's place, Sam spotting a movement near his condo. He stilled. "What the hell is going on?" he whispered.

Cat's body tensed. "I'm not sure. Someone is looking through your window."

Sam paused and watched a man rustle along the ground and peer in his window. From this distance and the insufficient light, he couldn't tell who it was but he had no doubt it was the same son of a bitch who had threatened Rio.

He fisted his hand, knowing he'd had enough already. It was time for him to do something about this asshole once and for all. No more hiding or keeping his distance, like his Director had suggested. This was going to be dealt with here and now, despite the fact that it could very well make tomorrow's headlines. No one messed with those he cared about and got away with it.

Sam grabbed his cell phone and handed it to Cat. "Get inside, lock the door, and call the police. Ask for Detective Doyle. I'll check it out."

Cat grabbed him. "Sam, no."

He saw concern in her eyes. "I'll be careful."

Sam moved into the shadows and quietly crept toward the guy. As he drew near, recognition hit, but the man's identity certainly didn't surprise him. It was none other than Eugene, the protestor who'd chased them into the alleyway.

In one hand Eugene fisted a crow bar, in the other he gripped some sort of bag. From the looks of things, it was obvious to Sam that the guy had every intention of kidnapping Rio.

Slowly, quietly, barely breathing, Sam snuck up behind him, hoping to catch Eugene off guard. Standing only inches from him he said, "Hey."

Eugene spun around, his eyes opened wide in surprise, but before he could get a word out, Sam punched him. His equipment flew from his grip and Sam kicked it away.

Hand cradling his eye, Eugene toppled like timber. "What the fu—"

His words fell off when Sam took a step toward him. Eugene scooted backwards and crouched against the brick wall, sinking into the shadows as Sam closed in on him. He held his palms up in a halting motion. "No. Don't."

Fisting his hands, Sam asked. "What the fuck do you think you're doing?"

"It's not my fault," Eugene blurted out.

Clenching his jaw, Sam glared at him. "What the fuck are you talking about? What do you mean it's not your fault?" Sam glanced around. "You're the only one I see here." Anger made his blood boil. Anger that this man had threatened someone he loved. "So help me God, if you ever lay a finger on Rio . . ."

"That reporter put me up to it."

Sam's jaw clenched. "You lying son of a bitch. Why would any reporter do that?"

"For the story."

Sam's nostrils flared. His hands shook. "What are you talking about?" he bit out through gritted teeth.

Eugene covered his swollen eye and groaned. "That reporter needed the story for a promotion," he rushed out. "I don't know all the details."

Jesus Christ. Sam's stomach twisted as Kale's words of warning echoed in his head. *"She's a reporter, Sam. She can't be trusted."*

Sam took a step closer, unable to believe what he was hearing.

Eugene backpedaled, trying to save his own ass, no doubt. "I needed the money. I wasn't going to hurt the chimp."

The sound of footsteps behind him gained his attention. He twisted around to see Cat standing there, cell phone in her hand.

Eyes wide, mouth open, her expression pained as she read the unanswered question in Sam's eyes. "Sam, it wasn't me."

He wanted to believe her, he really did, but Kale's words continued to haunt him. He felt a flash of doubt as he dredged up old fears and insecurities.

She stepped closer and reached out to him, her voice soft. "Sam, I know how this looks to you but trust me, it was Eric Hawkins who put Eugene up to this."

Hawk? Why would Hawk be on her story? None of this made sense.

"I saw the two of them talking yesterday just before Eugene chased us. I didn't mention it because I didn't want to worry you more. You had enough on your mind already and I had planned to investigate and get to the bottom of it for you."

He looked into her honest, honey-flecked eyes and wanted to believe everything she was telling him, *needed* to believe everything she was telling him. The alternative was too painful to consider.

His gaze brushed across her face as he took a moment to mull things over. Was he really going to believe some asshole protestor over Cat? The only woman who'd ever stood by him, who went against her own best interests for his, and stepped up to the plate to help him complete his assignment. He berated himself for thinking she'd do this, but old fears and insecurities were still far too close to the surface, making him feel far too vulnerable.

"Ask him, Sam."

Sam spun back around.

Eugene pressed himself farther into the wall. "Yeah, yeah, it was that reporter, Hawk. He's the guy you want, not me."

Sam caught hold of Cat's hand and watched her face relax as he drew her under his arms. "Did you call the police?"

She nodded. "They're on their way. I also called my boss and he's on his way to pay a visit to Eric Hawkins, to get to the bottom of this."

"I need to call my Director."

A short while later, after the police came and took Eugene to the station for questioning, Sam called and relayed the night's activities to his Director and then followed Cat back to her place. Armed with this new information, Director Smith planned on contacting the Board of Directors first thing in the morning to get the thumbs up for Sam to resume testing on the serum.

Once inside her condo, Cat turned to him and ran her fingers gently over his. Her eyes filled with tender concern. "Is your hand okay?"

Sam squeezed his fingers. "It's fine."

Cat took his hand in hers for a closer examination. As she lightly stroked her fingers over his, his heart swelled. God, he was crazy about her. How could he have believed for a split second that she'd do something so devious? Cat had integrity and character, and the way she stood by him warmed his soul.

"Go put some ice on it while I get changed. And while you're in the kitchen, pour us a drink. I could use it after that incident. There's a bottle of wine on the counter."

Sam dropped a soft kiss on her cheek and then made his

way to the kitchen. Ignoring the swelling in his hand, he found the wine and poured two glasses, hoping to meet her in the bedroom before she'd finished changing.

God, she'd only been out of his arms for a few minutes and he already missed her.

Just as he prepared to move down the hall, a letter on Cat's kitchen table drew his attention. As soon as he saw the words, the *Daily Press*, his heart pounded in his chest, his mouth went dry, and his bliss disappeared. Even though it was an invasion of her privacy, something compelled him to read the letter. He scanned the words once, then a second time, letting the reality of the situation sink in. A sick knot tightened his stomach. His blood ran cold, penetrating his bones.

A sound at the doorway drew his attention. He looked up to see Cat. His gaze flew to her face. God, how he longed for her. He watched her for a moment, his anger gaining momentum.

Her face tightened when he met her glance. Her lips thinned to a fine line, her eyes opened wide. She stood there, looking at him, gauging his reactions, knowing he'd read the letter from the *Daily Press*. She stared expectantly at him as though she was waiting for something, but for what, he didn't know.

Perhaps she was waiting for an offer to help her pack.

He shot her a sidelong glance and balled his fingers as his anger took hold. "How could you do this, Cat?" His voice came out a little unstable, a little gruff.

Seemingly surprised by his reaction, her head jerked with a start. "Do what?"

He cocked his head and struck out at her. "So who really put Eugene up to the kidnapping?" Wine sloshed over the side of his glass as he set it on the table. He grabbed the paper and held it up. "Who was the one looking for a promotion? Obviously you and Hawk had to be working together. Was the plan to cozy up to me to get the story?"

She reacted to the harshness in his voice. Eyes wide in astonishment, she shook her head and flinched at his harsh words. She tossed him a perplexed frown, a sadness in her eyes. "I told you it was Hawk." She seemed hurt. "I thought you believed that. I thought you trusted me."

Sam threaded his fingers through his hair, his eyebrows furrowed. "You want to talk about trust when all this time you were using me to get to bigger and better."

Pain and anger flashed in her eyes. "It's not true. I was there for you and I never once used you for personal gain. I would think you would know that. At least I had hoped you'd know that after we'd been so intimate and shared in something so special."

He grabbed the letter and flung it at her. "Why didn't you tell me about this?"

Her face softened. *"Sam . . ."* She reached out to him. "It's not what you think. If you'd just give me a minute to explain."

Sam backed up, not able to handle her warm, gentle touch. "I can't do this Cat, not again. Not ever again." Feeling suffocated, he had to get out of there, to get air. He couldn't stick around to listen to why she had to run away to bigger and better things. His stomach rolled. He bit back an ironic laugh.

Fuck! He glanced at his watch and took a deep breath.

He gave an angry shake of his head. Angry with himself for letting this relationship move beyond physical when he knew he didn't have what it took to keep her around. He hastily pushed past Cat and made his way to the door.

"It's late. I have to go get Rio."

Her voice was low and urgent. "Sam, wait."

Her words stopped him. He twisted back around, wanting to lash out again. "What? You need a lift to the airport?"

She winced at his harshness. "I wanted you to see the letter." She sounded edgy, emotional.

Sam shook his head in disbelief. "This is the reason you invited me back here, instead of going to my place. You wanted me to see this?" Christ, did she have some kind of cruel streak he didn't know about?

"I left the letter on the table for you to see. I wanted you to read it. I wanted you to ask me to stay." She stepped closer to him. "Don't you see? I needed to know I was more than a lab rat to you."

His stomach churned. He touched her arm, his fingers idly stroking her flesh. "I'd never do that, Cat. I'd never ask you to stay." With that he turned and walked out the door.

The look in his eyes before he left told her everything. She saw love, caring, and a little boy lost. Her heart swelled in her chest as tears pooled in her eyes.

Resisting the urge to go after him, she pulled in a breath and sorted through the events, taking a long time to reflect on Sam's childhood and insecurities. Understanding dawned in small increments. Understanding of where all that anger had come from, and why he had a hard time trusting her, why he'd lashed out at her.

It occurred to her that Sam had expected her to leave, just like everyone else in his life that he'd cared for and lost. Sam was too afraid to ask her to stay.

He might have just walked out on her but his reaction proved one thing. She was more than a lab rat to him. Otherwise the job offer wouldn't have mattered.

Cat glanced out her window to see Sam climb into his Jeep. Tears flowed down her cheeks as everything in her reached out to him. As hard as it was, she had to let him go.

Pleasure Exchange

Palms flat on the window, she watched him peel out of the parking lot, knowing he needed time to battle old ghosts, to find a way to heal, to find the courage to trust her.

And to find a way to come back on his own.

Chapter *11*

S am drove around for hours, with no specific destination in mind. As midnight came and went he found himself sitting outside Kale's house. He killed the ignition and just sat there, feeling numb, trying to sort through the night's events.

He glanced at the house. The lights were dimmed and it was late. Maybe he should just go home. He reached for the keys when the front door opened.

"Are you coming in or are you going to sit there all night?" Kale asked.

Feeling chilled, Sam climbed from the Jeep and scrubbed his hand over his jaw. "Did I wake you?"

"No, I was up with the baby, but now both my girls are asleep so keep it down."

Sam followed Kale inside and plunked himself down on

200

the sofa. The warmth of the house seeped into his skin. Blue rays fanned out from the television, providing the only source of light in the room.

"Beer?"

"Love one," Sam said.

Kale came back with two beers and handed one to Sam. Sam took a long pull as Kale grabbed the remote, muted the television, and sank back into his chair.

Kale got right to the point. "What's up, Sam?"

Sam shifted. "It's that obvious, is it?"

"Oh yeah. You look like shit."

How was that for blunt? "You think?"

Kale leaned forward. "Is it the reporter?"

"You could say that."

Kale pushed himself back into his seat. "Shit, Sam. I told you not to play with fire. What happened?"

Sam shook his head as a strange groan crawled out of his throat. He kept his voice low. "To be honest, I'm not sure. First, there was a threatening note; then, a protestor was at my house trying to kidnap Rio. He said Hawk put him up to it to get a good story for a promotion. Then I saw an interview letter on Cat's table." He was rambling and probably made no sense, but he didn't care.

"So let me get this straight. You think Cat and Hawk hired a protestor to kidnap Rio so she could get a promotion?"

Sam looked up from his beer. "Is that what I said?"

"Pretty much."

"Cat wasn't in on it, though."

Kale scoffed. "Are you kidding me? She's a reporter. Of course she was."

Sam's protective instincts kicked into high gear. "No, she wasn't." An equal measure of surprise and shock hit at the same time. It suddenly occurred to him that he was defending Cat and would continue to defend her with everything in him. "She's not like that, Kale. You don't know her the way I do. Don't say stuff like that about her."

He took a pause, considering everything over. Cat didn't have a manipulative bone in her body and he damn well knew it. He'd struck out at her earlier because she was leaving. The little boy lost cowering inside of him compelled him to hurt her the same way she'd hurt him. She might not have set Eugene up, but it didn't change the fact that she was leaving.

Him.

"Sam."

"Yeah?"

"You're protecting her."

"So?" Sam swallowed the rest of his beer and quietly set it on the coaster.

"And you're defending her," Kale added.

Sam arched his brow. "Your point?"

Kale grinned. "You're only protective of the people you love."

Planting his elbows on his knees, Sam rested his forehead in his palms and groaned. "I know."

After a long pause, Kale said, "So if you love her, why are you here?"

"Because she's leaving. Going to a job interview for her dream job in New York."

"I see."

Sam felt a flash of anger but kept his voice low, not wanting to wake Erin or the baby. He looked up and met Kale's glance. "No, you don't see."

"Then enlighten me."

"She wanted me to see the note. Wanted me to ask her to stay. Wanted to see if she was more than a lab rat to me."

"Then ask her."

Sam swallowed. "It's not so simple."

"Sure it is. You open your mouth and say, Cat, stay with me. Sometimes you have to fight for what you want, Sam. Look at me and Erin. I wasn't going down without a fight, and look how happy we are now."

Sam glanced at Kale and then perused the warm, loving environment. His heart twisted with envy. He felt a little vulnerable, a little raw, and a whole lot lonely. "What if she eventually leaves?"

Kale shrugged. "What if she doesn't? Are you going to throw this away because of a 'what if'? Because you're too chicken shit to give it a shot?"

Sam blew out a breath. "I guess that would be a dumb thing to do, wouldn't it?"

Kale grinned. "Pretty dumb, Sam. Even for you," he teased.

Cat stirred and tossed on her bed as she slipped in and out of a restless slumber. Her thoughts were on Sam, even in sleep. Wondering where he was and what he was doing. Every now and then she'd slip off the mattress and check the parking lot. It was nearing two in the morning, yet he hadn't come back.

Cat's stomach clenched and her heart ached, wondering if he ever would. Wondering if she'd made a huge mistake by letting him go.

Just as she was about to check her window again, her doorbell chimed.

Hope rushed through her as the sound filled her condo. She hurried down the hall and peeked through the peephole. Her breath stalled. She pulled open the door and came face-to-face with a very disheveled-looking Sam.

"Hi," he said.

Cat smoothed her hair off her face. It occurred to her, with her hair in a mess and her makeup smeared, she looked exactly like she did a few days ago on the picket line.

Great!

"Hi." Cat's heart swelled as she took in his pained expression.

Sam drove his hands deep into his pockets. "Can I come in?"

She nodded and gestured with her hands. God, she loved him so much it hurt.

After he walked through the doorway he turned to face her. His voice hitched as he swallowed. "This job, isn't it your dream?"

She shook her head and took a step toward him. "I thought it was, but I was wrong."

Sam pulled his hands from his pockets and brushed his fingers over her cheeks. He pitched his voice low. "Are you sure, Cat, because you need to be sure."

"I am sure." She could tell he was afraid to completely surrender his heart to her only to have her up and leave him, the way so many others had.

"If you give up your dream right now, Cat, you'll still leave. It will just be later."

"I was chasing the wrong dream, Sam. I was chasing someone else's dream."

He got quiet, worry etching his features as his fingers tangled through her hair.

"Talk to me, Sam."

After a long, agonized minute he said in a whispered

tone, "I'm worried that I don't have what it takes to keep you around."

Cat squeezed his arm, offering comfort and support. "I'm not like your mother or those other stand-ins your father brought home."

His brow puckered into a frown, conflicting emotions flickering in his eyes. "I want to be selfish and beg you to stay, I really do, but I want you to be happy."

She addressed his worries. "I learned something from you, Sam. I love my 'Cat on the Prowl' articles. I thought success came from writing hard-hitting news. I was wrong. You taught me that. Success comes from within and being happy doing what you're doing. I didn't realize how important my columns were, how much people enjoyed them, how much I enjoyed them."

He stepped closer to her, into her personal space. His hands dropped to her arms; his fingers idly stroking her flesh.

"I know you're afraid of emotional commitment, Sam. I've let go of old ideas and beliefs that have kept me from seeing what was right in front of my eyes all this time. What kept me from being happy. Now it's your turn."

Something in his expression changed. His face softened; his body relaxed. He leaned into her and gently kissed the side of her neck. He lingered there, breathing in her scent. Shivers of warm need left her shaking, unable to fill her lungs with air.

"Cat, sweetheart?"

She let out a little gasp as he gathered her into his arms and held her. She became hyperaware of the heat in his body as it pressed against hers. Lord, it felt so good to be held by him. Goose bumps pebbled her flesh.

"Yes?" she whispered.

He inched back and looked deep into her eyes. There was so much emotion and love in his gaze as it bore into her and stole her very next breath. "You were never just an experiment to me," he murmured low in his throat. "Ever."

She smiled up at him, her heart beating in a wild rush. "Good. You were never an experiment to me either, Sam."

He brushed his fingers over her cheeks and tucked her hair behind her ear. A gesture more intimate than a kiss.

"I love you, Cat. Will you stay with me? And we'll see where this all takes us."

His words drummed in her head as joy rushed through her bloodstream. Cat grinned and threw her arms around his neck. Her throat was tight with emotions.

"Oh Sam, I thought you'd never ask."

After he hugged her, he inched back and frowned. "I'm sorry for accusing you of hiring Eugene. Deep down I knew you'd never do that. I lashed out in anger. I guess I still have a lot of things to work through."

She touched his cheek then signed the words *I love you*, the way Rio had taught her. When he signed the words back, her heart soared like a leaf caught in an updraft. "And I'll be here to help you work through them. Because, Sam York, you've got what it takes to keep me around. Forever."

Epilogue

One year later

Cat smoothed down her sleek black cocktail dress and took a seat beside her husband at the head table. Sitting in the gorgeous banquet room inside a posh hotel overlooking the city, she perused the crowd gathered to celebrate Sam's success with the new female libido enhancer. During the course of the evening, Cat and Sam mingled with their friends Laura and Jay Cutler and Erin and Kale Alexander. The five scientists were in secret talks about a new experiment. Sam promised as soon as he knew more, he'd let her in on it. And if all went well, she'd be the first to report it to the public through her "Cat on the Prowl" article.

Fortunately, since Hawk had been fired, things were much better at the office now. Amanda Stone had been hired, taking over the "Eye of the Hawk" column. They were still working on a catchy title for her.

The sound of Director Reginald Smith tapping his spoon on his wine glass drew everyone's attention. Cat smiled, her heart swelling in her chest as she watched Sam rise and accept a plaque from the Director for his successes at the lab.

Of course, the Director hadn't always been so pleased with Sam. After he found out Sam and Cat had spent an entire week testing the new serum before approval had been given, he'd nearly kicked Sam's ass to the curb. But since the Grant Governing Board stepped in and presented the Director with an abundance of grant money, he'd softened around the edges.

God, Sam looked incredibly handsome in his tux as he accepted the plaque and glanced around the room. As his gaze settled on Cat, the love she felt for him rushed over her like a wind storm. In turn, his blue eyes twinkled with the love he felt for her in return.

Sam held the plaque high. "To future experiments," he said, winking at Cat.

Cat grinned back. She really had no idea what they planned to test next. She just hoped Sam asked her to be his guinea pig.

After Sam gave his speech, he returned to his seat beside her.

"You did great," she whispered in his ear.

He smiled. "Thanks." Just then their server came with dessert. As Cat glanced at her plate, her whole body moistened and her blood pressure soared.

As she took in the sight of her delicious cake, drizzled in chocolate sauce, and surrounded by fresh fruit, her mouth watered, but not for her dessert.

"Um, Sam."

"Yeah?"

"Are you hungry?"

He gave her a perplexed frown. Cat picked up the orange slice from her plate and drew it into her lips. She squeezed the juice into her mouth before popping it inside.

She watched Sam's throat work as he swallowed. "Jesus, Cat." He glanced around and adjusted his pants. "What the hell are you trying to do to me? These dress pants are as unforgiving as scrubs."

"Are you feeling . . . *uncomfortable?*"

"Hell, yeah."

She shook her head in dismay. "Well, we can't have that, Sam. You can't be uncomfortable at your own party."

His grin turned wicked, his eyes smoldering. Cat felt her panties grow damp as his eyes latched upon her cleavage. God, she would never tire of the way he looked at her with such passion, such love. The two had grown so close over the past year, their relationship growing stronger and stronger by the day.

His voice dropped an octave. "I think you're right, Cat. Why don't you grab that orange slice and meet me in the hall? I spotted a storage closet there earlier."

"A storage closet, Sam. Isn't that a little risky? A little naughty?"

His lips twitched and the fire in his eyes licked her from head to toe. "That's never stopped us before."

Her pulse leapt as his hand touched her thigh under the table. Without pause, Cat raised her voice. "If you'll all excuse me, I have to make a quick trip to the little girl's room." She hastily disposed of her napkin and rushed from the room.

Cat made her way to the hall. Her body fairly shook with excitement. In no time at all, she found the room Sam had staked out. She pushed open the door and catalogued her surroundings. As she made a move to enter, she felt a large hand splay out over the small of her back. Her whole body moistened as she absorbed Sam's warmth.

He put his mouth close to her ear. His warm breath made her shiver with longing. "Are you looking for something, ma'am?" he asked, urging her forward, closing the door behind them.

Both love and desire raced through her as she twisted around to face him. His eyes clouded with passion as they moved over her face. Cat moistened her lips. "Yes, sir, as a matter of fact I am." Her hand traveled over his chest and lower until she reached his cock.

She squeezed.

He groaned.

"Ah, I believe I found what I was looking for."

"Christ, that feels good." His cock jolted and grew beneath her hands. Her lips found his. She drew his scent into her lungs as they exchanged kisses. Cat's nipples quivered as Sam's hands touched her all over, exploring her every curve. Fire burned through her veins.

"God, I love you so much, babe," Sam whispered into her mouth. "I can't get enough of you." His hands cupped her breasts and squeezed.

Cat moaned and inched back. Impatience seeped through her. "Please, Sam, I want your cock in me. Now," she murmured with effort.

Sam hiked her dress up over her hips and pushed her panties to the side. His thumb opened her sex lips. She shivered under his touch.

"Are you ready for that?" He stroked her sex and groaned with satisfaction. "You're so wet and so very, very ready." His voice was full of want.

Sam planted a warm kiss on her mouth before he sank to his knees. He snapped the thin elastic on her panties and tucked them into his pocket.

"Oh, my," Cat whispered. He slid his hands over her thighs, his mouth brushing against her skin. His touch went right through her. Her breasts felt swollen and hot. She arched into him as desire bombarded her body. She shook with sexual need.

"Sam . . . please." She gave a broken gasp.

Hands shaking, Cat raked her fingers through his hair as his mouth found her clit and greedily drew it in between his lips. She gripped his head and held him there as she rode his tongue furiously. Her pussy muscles spasmed as he sucked her in deeper.

Sam stroked her sex with his tongue and plunged into her damp core, making her wild with need. Her breath grew shallow and her whole body convulsed as he nibbled and nipped and brought her to the edge.

Her pussy muscles clenched and undulated with the rippling approach of an orgasm. Tilting her head back, Cat bit down on her lip and moaned. Their aroused aromas mingled and filled the small space.

Moments before her orgasm tore through her, Sam climbed out from between her legs, backed her up until she was pressed against the wall, and tore off his pants. His hands found her hips as his thick cock probed her opening.

"I need to fuck you, Cat." There was so much urgency and emotion in his voice.

The love she saw in his eyes nearly made her weep. She touched his cheek. Warm familiarity curled around her. She gave a breathy moan. "Then fuck me," she whispered.

In one quick thrust he impaled her, the depth of penetration making her quiver. Cat sucked in a tight breath.

Together they established a rhythm, each giving and taking, emotionally and physically, as he buried himself in her.

Sam plunged deeper, driving into her with fierce need, building her orgasm, touching the spot deep inside her that made her quake. His mouth found hers and ravished her with dark hunger.

Sam's hand slipped between their bodies. As soon as he pressed his finger to her clit and stroked her with expertise, she exploded with a hot flow of release. "Oh God," she cried out, her hands biting into his flesh.

"That's it, Cat. Come for me." His voice hitched and she knew he was right there with her. "I love how you come for me, babe."

Cat felt his cock pulse and throb with his release. They held each other for a long moment, riding out the pleasure, never wanting it to end.

When his cock slipped from her opening, Cat gave a contented sigh and nestled against him. "That was perfect."

He circled his arms around her and held her tight. "It's always perfect with you, Cat."

Cat inched back and looked into his eyes. Her lips twitched in amusement. "Only one problem, Sam."

"One problem?"

She shook her head. "I forgot the orange slice."

Sam's laugh was rough. His gaze shifted to her breasts. "I guess you know what that means." He brushed the rough pad of his thumb over her kiss-swollen lips.

She arched one brow, curious. "No, what?" she asked, already knowing the answer to that question.

"Looks like we're going to have to do this again."

Cat gave a low throaty chuckle as Sam's lips closed over hers. "Well hell, the things I have to do in the name of love."

CATHRYN FOX

A multi-published author in the romance genre, Cathryn has two teenagers who keep her busy and a husband who is convinced he can turn her into a mixed martial arts fan. Cathryn can never find balance in her life and is always trying to keep up with emails, Facebook, Pinterest, and Twitter. She spends her days writing page-turning books filled with heat and heart, and loves to hear from her readers.

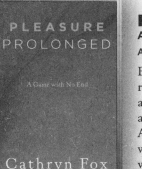

JUL 1 5 2013